Operation Flamenco

Operation Flamenco

Mark Simmons

Published By: Lulu.com
Cover by: Shutterstock. Fernando Cortes
ISBN:978-0-244-80089-5

To my Lovely

'Bear in mind, Sancho, that one man is no more than
another, unless he does more than another.'
Don Quixote La Mancha
Miguel Cervantes

'Dance is the ritual of immortality.'
Shah Asad Rizvi

Prologue

Friday 10 October 1986
Sheremetyevo International Airport Moscow

The Ilyushin IL-86 wide bodied air liner of the Special Purpose Aviation Division, from the Air Force base at Chkalovsky, stood waiting away from the main terminal building used by the commercial traffic at Sheremetyevo Airport. The auxiliary engines had been started prior to starting the four main Kuznetsov NK-86 engines, the flight plan to Reykjavik, Iceland logged and ready, flying time from Moscow seven hours, distance 2,100 miles.

On board waiting for takeoff Mikhail Gorbachev, General Secretary of the Communist Party of the Soviet Union, his wife Raisa and his handpicked staff, about to set off to meet President of the United States Ronald Reagan to discuss the reduction of nuclear weapons.

Age fifty-five Gorbachev had become General Secretary in March; with the help of the KGB he had purged the Brezhnev old guard, only a month later he had promoted KGB Chairman Viktor Chebrikov to the Politburo. However not all those within the KGB were enamoured with Gorbachev and his policy of *perestroika* (restructuring) and *glasnost* (openness).

One of Gorbachev's aides comes forward to speak with him in low tones. He nods and smiles 'a little delay' he says to Raisa. He notices two Zil-41047 limousines pull up beside the aircraft; the boarding steps are wheeled back into place. Viktor Chebrikov the KGB's spymaster and several men get out of the cars and wait to come on board.

One month earlier.

Chapter 1

Friday 5 September 1986

Rob Nicolson sat in the centre seat of three on a charter tourist flight to Malaga. The large woman of about fifty sat in the aisle seat, Beryl Hope was gripping Rob's right hand as the Boeing 737-300 accelerated along the main runway at Bournemouth. Then they were off the ground in a steep climb, Beryl let out a cry more like a squawk and the pressure of her grip increased.

'Stupid bitch' said her husband Horace, sat in the window seat gazing down at the ground that was fast receding. By the smell of his breath he had already sunk a few beers and it was not yet 10 a.m. 'Less chance of a crash in one of these than in a motor but she don't listen.'

'Now Horace' said Beryl 'it's alright for you. But some people don't like flying, now what's it called?'

'Aviophobia I think' said Rob; she was still clutching his hand.

'That's it Duncan.'

As the plane began to level out, her grip relaxed, and then she placed Rob's hand back on his knee with a parting friendly pat. 'I think I'll be OK now.'

'Until we land' sniggered Horace.

Rob groaned to himself thinking *why does it happen to me?* Still it was only a two hour flight. He closed his mind to her prattle, just nodding now and then, adding the odd 'right' or 'is that so.'

9

The passport inside his jacket was in the name of Duncan Forbes Dixon. It was an easy job he had been given, although his last job was supposed to have been easy and had almost cost him his life. The trip to the Costa del Sol was more in the nature of R and R, and to keep him out of the limelight for a while. Until the IRA moved onto something else or that's the jargon he had been given. He viewed it with some trepidation as likely to be a complete bore.

He had been lucky in Liverpool's Toxteth Cemetery. The Irishman had been an amateur choosing the wrong time and wrong weapon. He had hit him twice out of three shots fired from the Walter PPK not bad for a pistol and the first time he had used it. But maybe all three should have hit at fifteen yards. He felt no remorse over the Irishman, it was kill or be killed. Major Lanyon had debriefed him on his return to London. He was sat bolt upright behind his desk, in shirt sleeves, the white shirt's starched creases were arrow straight, the Coldstream Guards tie perfectly knotted.

'No good going back to your flat Nicolson. In fact later might be an idea to sell it and get yourself a new pad. As the Director mentioned to you we are sending you to the Costa del Sol for your health now at last you have agreed to join the firm. And how about that woman of yours?'

'Dawn Jenkins, sorry she won't play ball Major, but she has agreed to go to Southampton and stay with her aunt. She doesn't trust the firm.' *Or me anymore* he thought.

'Pity, never understand people not trusting us, it would have been better to have you both in the same place, but we will get the local Bobbies to keep an eye on her.' He jotted a note down in a pad with a fountain pen. 'Chances are the

Provo's have enough on their plate to bother with her. It will be you they are really interested in. Right we have a new identity for you.' He took a passport out of a desk drawer, briefly flicked through it. 'Not bad' he said sliding it across the desk.

Rob picked it up and opened it; he found it odd to see his face staring back at him under a different name. Duncan Forbes Dixon, occupation property consultant.

'You don't have to do much over there. We have a small villa rented for you for six months place called Nerja an hour north of Malaga. Just keep your head down. Now you are signed up you can draw money at the local bank. Don't go over the top. Julie has all the details. You take a tourist flight from Bournemouth, catch the train down there. Any questions Nicolson?'

'What about the job over there?'

'Yes on that! Commander Matthew Styles, one of your lot, a Navy man. Served in Naval Intelligence during the war, worked for six after that then with us about ten years, retired and went to live in Spain. Heard little from him until a few weeks ago, insisted we send someone out to see him. One of the local FO chaps from the consulate went to see him; he lives out there alone, in his seventies now. Sounds like he's gone doolally, got angry chased the consulate fellow off. Broke up with his wife soon after going out there, she came back, died in eighty-two.'

'Any other relatives?' asked Rob

'Good question Nicolson, Julie' he shouted.

'Yes Major' said Julie red faced at the door.

'Commander Styles has he any living relatives?'

'Yes a daughter lives in Exmouth Devon they seem estranged, maybe she took her mother's side when they split up.'

It struck Rob that Lanyon did not seem at all up to date on Commander Styles.

'Time is pressing Nicolson go out there with Julie she will fill you in. See you when you get back. Close the door on your way out.'

Nothing like being dismissed thought Rob. In the outer office Julie gave him Styles's file to read. He sat in a comfortable armchair. The file was thin. He had joined the navy in 1934 Britannia Naval College good marks. Then served on various ships. 1939 joined Naval Intelligence, NI man in Gibraltar 1941-43. After the war joined MI6, married Miriam Wardlaw in 1956, daughter born 1959, and 1960 joined MI5. Retired 1967 moved to Spain same year. In 1970 Miriam and daughter were back in the UK. All factual details but told no real story.

'Did they get divorced Julie?'

'If it's not there I doubt it, can check for you if you like, and send it on?'

'Thank you I don't know if it will make much difference but you never know. And what about the daughter do we have anything on her, doesn't even seem to be a name here?'

'No problem' she made a note on her pad. 'One thing did strike me having read a lot of these, there are no black marks everything is "excellent" or "exemplary" he seems almost too good to be true.'

'The major doesn't seem concerned' said Rob closing the file getting up and passing it back. 'Thanks Julie.'

She gave him an envelope with tickets, details of the villa and bank details and some money. 'Need you to sign the chit for that lot.'

Rob did so. 'Thanks again' he said.

'Nice to be appreciated' she said. 'You take care Rob the sun is strong out there.'

Walking along the corridor to the stairs and the way out of the Gower Street MI5 building he reflected on the distinct impression he got Julie was not fond of Lanyon. He found it no surprise with the Major's overbearing nature. *Maybe that's why he got stuck at Major* thought Rob, often a dead end rank in the Army.

Going down the stairs he came across the Director Leo Hawthorne on his way up dressed in a scruffy tweed jacket and baggy trousers.

'Nicolson, good to see you off to the Costa's, Norm filled you in' he said gasping for breath.

'Yes sir fly out tomorrow.'

'Grand, keep your head down and you should be back in a few weeks, can't stay chatting have a good trip. You know I do this for exercise think it will kill me one day' he said and continued up the stairs puffing and blowing.

Chapter 2

4 September P.M.

While Rob Nicolson was sound asleep in his Bournemouth Hotel room the night before his flight to Malaga, Commander Matthew Styles lay awake in his bed. He gazed at the ceiling watching the full Moon reflected onto it. He always slept with the curtains open. He had just about calmed down after the visit of the Foreign Office man from the consulate in Malaga to his Villa *Ocean View* in Almunecar. Why had they sent such an idiot like that *bloody office junior?* he thought. He knew even a younger man from the Firm would be difficult to convince. Although he hoped would be better trained.

'Are you sure it was him, old man?' the toffee nosed twerp had said.

'It had to be I shared a cabin with him for long enough on the *Hood'* he had replied.

The good old *Hood*, not that Martin Judd was at the bottom of the Atlantic with the other one thousand four hundred and fifteen poor devils, only three had got off after she went down so fast in the Battle of the Denmark Strait. No Judd had died years before that. He had been there when they buried him with full military honours in Barcelona. The ship had docked to take on refugees trying to escape the civil war, to Palma or was it France he could not remember but he remembered Martin Judd. Shore parties had been out and about the city. During one of these

14

Judd had been caught in a Nationalist air raid. *Bloody hell I led the burial party.*

Yet a few days ago he had seen him in an Almunecar supermarket. Not only seen him but heard him speaking Russian. There was a stunning woman with him, tall, elegant, blonde about thirty, who he was talking to, they seemed intimate filling a trolley with groceries. He knew it was Russian, but his Russian was not good enough to pick up much. But did she call him *deda* he was not sure but knew that was Papa or father.

And the other thing was all those years ago Styles had been convinced, while serving with Judd in the *Hood,* that he was a Red. He was vocal enough about it, in the aftermath of the Invergordon Mutiny.

Styles had got out of the supermarket before them and outside he had waited for them to come out. The trolley they had was full to the brim, they had trouble with one of the wheels but both of them managed to steer it to a black Mercedes saloon. The woman opened the boot and they loaded everything in. Judd returned the trolley as the woman backed the car out.

He followed them in his Ford Fiesta. It was years since he had done this sort of thing but he knew the form. Not to follow too close, hang back; try to keep some traffic between you and the target. He tailed the Mercedes about five miles north along the coast road the N340, then they turned inland onto the Granada road the N323. About a mile or so later branched off onto a b road and at a Y junction they turned left onto a track. Styles slowed right down he barely had them in sight. Then they stopped opposite a gate which began to open, *electric job* he thought. Styles stopped he watched the Mercedes disappear behind trees that screened a large villa he could just see the roof line above the trees. The gate started shutting. He was reluctant to go closer he turned around. He began to doubt himself maybe it wasn't Judd.

Back home Styles went through his photo albums from the Hood. A meticulous man he had them all in order. It did not take him long to find group pictures of crew members of the *Hood* dating back to 1938. He found Judd in two of them and marked under him with a small cross. Judd had even been given a posthumous mention in dispatches for rescuing people from a burning building. According to witnesses and the petty officer of the shore party he had gone back in a second time but the building had collapsed. He scratched his head; it was nearly fifty years ago. 'Well there is only one way to find out.'

With a new film in his camera and a pair of binoculars two days later he drove back to the track and parked his car on the grass verge. He cut across country toward the villa. There was a six foot high chain link fence running right the way around it. But the links in the fence were quite wide enough to accommodate the lens of the camera. There was quite a bit of coming and going around the garden and veranda doors his best view was of the back of the house. He began to think he might run out of film he had taken 28 out of 36. When at last Judd appeared he took three of him. Satisfied he made his way back to his car careful to remain in cover, he opened the boot to put the camera and binoculars away.

'Trouble Senor?'

'Styles turned around a tall man stood a few feet away. Muscular, young age under thirty, dressed in shorts and a T shirt his eyes hidden by dark glasses. The accent wasn't

16

Spanish. He had an unfriendly looking Alsatian on a short lead that growled at Styles until the man jerked the lead and the dog lay down.

'No not at all, bird watching' Styles said and wondered how long he had been watching him.

'Here, I have not heard say of anything special?'

'Oh yes the yellow tailed buzzard but none around today, but that's how it goes with us twitchers.

'Twitchers what is this?'

The man had struggled with the English word. 'Ah, that' he laughed 'that's a British word for bird watchers.'

'You are British?'

'That's right and on my way.' Styles shut the boot got into the car started the engine and turned around and drove back the way he had come. In the rear view mirror he could see the man and dog standing in the middle of the track watching him.

Why did I say Yellow tailed Buzzard if they check on that they will smell a rat, it was obvious he was from the house, should have hidden the car better you're losing your touch he thought.

The next day he got the photos developed in a two hour tourist shop. Some were blurred others had heads missing or he had missed the person altogether, but the ones of Martin Judd were clear, and there was no doubt in his mind it was Martin Judd. That afternoon he telephoned the British Consulate in Malaga told them he was former MI5 and wanted to see someone pronto.

After that he went out into the garden pottering, always helped him relax. He had a big garden which he was finding difficult to maintain. He had a handy man come round once a fortnight for a clear up and trim, *short back and sides* Styles called it. Roy could turn his hands to most things; he was a cockney an amiable character.

That afternoon he did not feel his time in the garden was quite so much of the pleasure it usually was. He knew most of the cars his neighbours had. None of them had a black Mercedes with tinted windows which was parked across the street. But that Russian woman with Martin had one; he wished he had taken the registration number. Were they watching him? How would they have found out where he lived? He was sure nobody had followed him. *Fool* he thought *my registration number grease a few palms they would soon get my address.*

The meeting with the man from the FO had gone badly he was not really interested. Other than if Styles had wanted to sell the bungalow. 'I don't want to sell the bloody house, haven't you been listening to me?' Styles had exploded.

'I will send a report to the security services rest assured Commander Styles, but I think maybe your imagination...'

'Get out you moron' and Styles had shown him the door. Typical he noted there was no black Mercedes parked across the road while he had been there.

Styles went out the next morning to the post office and sent the negatives of the film he had taken at the villa and the old photos of Judd to his daughter Linda in Exmouth. He could not remember the old MI5 address and they must have moved by now. He put in a note for MI5 and asked her to find their address and forward it on, he was sure she would do it.

That night he lay awake until the early hours, but at last he drifted off into a troubled sleep. It was as if he was floating,

18

then all of a sudden he could feel the ship vibrating under his feet, they were working up to full speed into the teeth of a gale. He was at his action station in the damage control centre. And then he could feel the main guns firing hurling the 15inch shells twenty miles, but only the forward turrets as they strove to close the range to the German ships. Then he could hear incoming fire screaming like an express train. Then there was a hit a lighter shell and the boat deck was on fire. Commander Damage Control directed parties to tackle the fire. He was moving through the ship following them yet it was as if he was barely moving, as if his feet were in treacle. There were loud explosions rocking the ship as ready use four inch ammunition lockers blew up. The ship was hit again by something altogether bigger as if shaken by a giant hand. Wounded she began to list port, but did not stop, Styles expected her to right herself but she kept rolling. There was a muffled explosion deep within her, and then the great ship broke in two. He was swept off his feet by a wave of icy water. He tried to kick forward to find a way out, the lights had gone out, and he could not breathe.

He opened his eyes something was pressing down on his face; he was suffocating he was pinned down. He tried to kick but it was no use. Where am I he thought? A sharp pain grabbed at his chest. He could not breathe he tried to move his head but could not. Then he felt the icy water again and he was sinking, sinking away.

Chapter 3

'Bye bye Duncan' someone was shouting, Rob saw Beryl and Horace were waving in his direction beside a trolley loaded high with their luggage. He could not get used to using another name. He waved back from the baggage reclaim where he was waiting. *Bugger off* he thought and wondered *how the hell had they got their gear so quickly?*

He had gone through the same performance with Beryl on landing as on takeoff. She may have been a tad better after being lubricated by two large gin and tonics. She had tried to pump him about what he would be doing in Spain. 'Perhaps we can meet up' she said giving him a wink and an extra squeeze of his hand.

Rob side stepped that one, telling her he would be heading north straight away, looking at properties for investors and clients in the UK. Knowing the Hopes were heading south for a family reunion.

A single suitcase and a holdall reclaimed he was through Spanish immigration with a bare glance at his passport. Reaching the exit area he began looking for car rental, but was surprised to see a man holding up a sign with, Mr Duncan Dixon written on it in large letters. *What now* he groaned *nothing like advertising my arrival.* The man holding it was dressed in a well cut blue suit mid twenties maybe a shade younger every inch an Englishman.

'I'm Duncan Dixon' said Rob moving up to him.

'Right Sir Ian Hamilton from the Consulate we have....'

'Stop right there Ian' said Rob interrupting him 'let's go somewhere less public.'

'Oh yes, right'oh of course mum's the word.' He led him outside. 'My car's in the car park.'

'That will do fine' said Rob.

Hamilton unlocked a Fiat 131; Rob put his gear on the back seat and got in.

'Right Mr Dixon...'

'Let's see some ID first' said Rob.

'Yes, yes of course not familiar with you cloak and dagger fellows.'

The ID checked out, his photo looked something like him.

'OK Ian now what is this all about?'

'It is Commander Styles, I'm sorry to say he died last night. We informed your people as soon as we knew they said to meet you at the airport. I assume your mission is over?'

'That's all they said?'

'Yes sir.'

'Hmm, OK do you know what Styles died of?'

'I did speak to the local doctor on the telephone natural causes, heart attack. But officially we have to wait for the Don's coroner's report.'

'One of your people did see him while he was alive?'

'Yes me again, I get all the odd jobs.' He reddened 'not that I mean....'

Rob interrupted 'what happened with Styles?'

'Damn near threw me out got angry.'

'What did he want?' said Rob getting irritated by Hamilton.

'As far as I could understand, he had seen someone off a ship he was on, he was a navy man. Mind you that was fifty years ago. I'm not sure if he was a deserter or, or....'

'Or what?' snapped Rob.

'I think he felt this fellow, Martin Judd, should be dead.'

'Really' said Rob thinking for a moment. 'My people did not want me to check it out?'

'They left no instructions sir.'

'Right Ian I had best look into it. But first I will pick up my hire car and go onto my place in Nerja.'

'Yes your people gave us your address over here.'

So much for my presence being secret Rob thought knowing the working of offices from his Merton Council days, now half the Consulate knew he was here. 'Can you pick me up about ten tomorrow and we will go round to Styles's place, will that be OK?'

'I should think so sir.'

'Don't call me Sir, Duncan will be fine' said Rob.

By the time Rob got his hire car and reached his bungalow on the El Capistrano estate of holiday homes on the outskirts of Nerja it was gone five in the afternoon. The key was under a plant pot there was no need for him to go to the estate office. *It's no villa* thought Rob laughing out loud. The place was small with one bedroom and an open plan kitchen and lounge, it was clean and spick and span. There was even a small hamper of essentials. It would suit him fine, better than a big place. Rob made himself a cup of coffee and unpacked then showered. About seven he set off for the town which was within walking distance.

He got some Tapas and a beer in a bar, where the locals were watching football.

After an hour and finding the match boring he took a walk along the seafront. The views from the Balcon de Europa up and down the coast were impressive even in twilight. Not that it did much for his spirits he was already feeling the pangs of loneliness and he had just arrived. There were a lot of people promenading, couples arm-in-arm, which made him think of Dawn. She was right of course in that she would never have rested while he worked for the Firm. Yet this was the only way out. But he too was not going to hide for the rest of his life, with a new ID, from the IRA, the fact that Dawn would not do it for him for a few months meant it was over between them.

He headed back toward the village. He had seen a supermarket on the way to the town he thought he might get a bottle of something stronger, and a few odds and ends. He began making a mental list.

Walking up the hill back toward the estate and supermarket he came across the Hotel Nerja Club, its room rates were on display outside also the notice stated, 'Entertainment open to Non-Residents. Flamenco Tonight' *Why not* he thought just a night cap *won't stay long.* At the bar he got a coffee and brandy. He found an empty table and warmed to the atmosphere the place soon began to fill up, most were British as far as he could tell, come in for the nine o'clock Flamenco show. Waiters were moving around the tables keeping the guests well lubricated. Rob ordered another brandy. Soon a young couple had taken the empty seats at his table.

Two men dressed all in black one with a guitar came onto the dance floor they took up position in an alcove where

23

there was an electric organ. They were followed a few moments later by three girls, dressed also in predominantly black dresses that tightly hugged their bodies reaching right down to the floor, ending with a frill of red and yellow. They carried brightly coloured fans and castanets. Their long black inky hair was tied back severely to their heads; behind their ears were pinned red flowers. There was a glow about them, an eastern pride to their beauty. One was taller and slightly heavier by a pound or two than the other two who looked like sisters. Next a surly looking brute dressed again all in black stamped arrogantly onto the floor, the crowd grew silent.

By then in 1986 Flamenco could be found all over Spain it was no longer the preserve of the Gypsies of Seville or Jerez or even of Andalusia. It had become a strong tourist attraction throughout the country.

The guitar player began strumming his instrument. The man in the centre of the dance floor began by drawing from deep inside himself a guttural song with long drawn out syllables; he pointed one foot and then began a slow heel and toe movement, his clapping hands joined in, the tapping striking feet adorned with high heeled ankle boots rose to a staccato rhythm getting faster and faster. Then the girls came onto the floor whirling and heel tapping, hopping and spinning and using their castanets joining the rhythm. Rob was swept up in the pain, sorrow and happiness of the performance. They went through several routines that were wildly applauded by the audience. Then the girls turned to the crowd dragging unwilling members of the audience out onto the floor to join in. This was below the dignity of the *bailaor* the male dancer who had disappeared.

Rob full of the brandy of Jerez was more than a willing participant, joining in with abandon, the stamping and posing. He was cheered by the crowd and clapped off by the girls. All too soon it was over. Rob downed a final double brandy at the bar his head still ringing from the thrill of the Flamenco.

As soon as he got outside Rob knew he had drunk too much. Still it was not far to his bungalow. And he had enjoyed the evening. 'Supposed to be keeping a low profile' he muttered.

'Ha, you were good man, a natural.'

Rob turned to find the bigger of the three girl flamenco dancers behind him. He stopped to let her catch up. She looked different in jeans and a T shirt with her hair down around her shoulders, carrying a bag presumably with her costume inside.

'I loved it' said Rob trying not to slur his words 'good way of letting off steam.'

'Right feller, where are you heading?'

There was something about her accent he could not quite put his finger on, her English was excellent. 'Over there' he pointed to El Capistrano village. Up ahead he could see the supermarket was closed now.

'Snap' the girl said.

'You're not Spanish are you?' said Rob.

'No boy'oh from the valleys me. But my father was Spanish, an orphan evacuated in the Civil War, ended up in Wales. Stayed, married my mother and I am the result of that union Caroline Gomez.'

'Caroline, Duncan Dixon at your service' for some reason he could not fathom he hated lying to her in particular. 'You come out here to work?'

25

'That's right this is my third season, its good money if tiring. What about you Duncan, holiday?'

They carried on walking toward the crossing. 'Not exactly' said Rob 'more a working break, looking at properties for clients in the UK.' More lies he thought.

They crossed the road together, a busy main road during the day but largely deserted of traffic at this time of night other than for the odd taxi.

'Must be expensive staying here?' said Rob.

'No it's not so bad you know, four of us share and they give us a discount for a long booking. Sunday we have no performance, having a barbeque and paella why not join us Duncan?' She had stopped beside a path leading to one of the bungalows it looked bigger to Rob than the one he had.

'I'm here' she said.

'Right I'm up near the top' said Rob he noted her number, 79.

'Will see you Sunday Duncan?'

'Yes' said Rob 'look forward to that.'

Rob continued walking seemed a nice girl he thought, mid twenties maybe a bit older.

Chapter 4

He was awake as usual by eight; he had a dry mouth and thick head. Getting up slowly he guzzled two glasses of bottled water from the fridge. Then he got under the shower letting the water cascade down over him for several minutes. *Bugger the water shortage* he thought.

Dressed, he went to the supermarket and got some essentials for his larder. He breakfasted on some fresh croissants. Gloom descended on him again, he began thinking of Dawn, if only she had come with him. Instead now he was wedded to the Firm, hiding from IRA assassins. *No good drinking yourself into oblivion.* 'Have to bury myself in work, and if that leads nowhere maybe I'll become a Flamenco dancer nimble on my pins and sod the Firm' he said to the empty room.

Hamilton arrived ten minutes early. Rob found him depressingly cheerful which he found irritated him.

'Almunecar, where have I heard that name before?' Rob asked as they set off in the Fiat.

'No doubt Laurie Lee, *As I walked out one midsummer morning* he called it Castillo in the book to protect people there after the Civil War.'

'Yes your right' Rob recalled reading the book years ago.

It took them half an hour to reach Sea View, from which you could barely see the sea. Maybe when it was first built, but some high rise building had blocked that out. It was a big sprawling place. Hamilton had a key supplied by the

27

police or 'Dons' as he liked to refer to anything Spanish. He let them into a large hall leading onto a long corridor.

'What are we looking for Duncan?'

'I have no idea; I'm just trying to get a feel for the man.' Rob started in the kitchen Hamilton followed him. There was little food in the place. Some milk in the fridge that smelled like it had gone off he tipped it down the sink and ran some water. A couple of tins, half a mouldy loaf in the bread bin. He opened some drawers, nothing other than what you would expect.

There were four bedrooms off the main hall all to the left. The main one where the body had been found the bed laid unmade the sheets all crumpled.

'Who found him?' said Rob.

'His handyman comes around about once a fortnight.'

'Right rather lucky, so if he had not been due, it would have been us.'

'Yes I suppose so' said Hamilton.

They moved to the study on the right of the corridor. Rob examined the bookcase, novels mostly thrillers, some Dickens.

'This is where I saw him' said Hamilton.

'Right' said Rob 'notice anything different?'

'Like what?'

'Well I wasn't here was I.' Rob sat behind the desk and started opening drawers and rummaged about he looked at cheque books and bank statements. 'Reasonably well off' he observed. He got up, on a shelf above a cabinet a picture of a smiling woman maybe thirty, on the same shelf a model of a ship, some sort of battleship he thought two funnelled job. On another shelf were a stack of photo albums, in jumbled positions. He took one down, opened it on the desk, on the front page in neat handwriting 1960-1962. Looked like family stuff some beach outings. He took another down 1943-1945, groups of naval officers wrens as well, must have been a shore establishment.

'This one is 1957-1959' said Hamilton flicking through it.

'Notice something odd about this?' said Rob.

'No can't say I do.'

'He has gone to a lot of trouble to date the books, and several of the photos have captions as well, a neat job. Neat man by the feel of the place, yet these albums are stacked on the shelves any old how.' Rob opened 1938 and flicked through it stopping at a page. 'Odd again' he said showing it to Hamilton 'two missing, look pulled out broken the small corners that hold them in. Says below ships officers Hood 1938, bet that's the Hood over there. Bear with me Ian let's take them all off and put them back in date order.'

It took them a few minutes there were over forty volumes, when they had finished they fitted perfectly with a little room to spare.

'Now what does that tell us Ian?'

'Someone has had a look at them other than Commander Styles.'

'Got it in one' said Rob. He went back to the desk and sat down. 'What else is staring us in the face?' He opened the drawer where the bank statements were again. There were a pile of receipts he handed some to Hamilton, while he looked at others.

'Got fuel four days ago' said Hamilton.

'Right good so he has been out in the car.'

'Local garage too. Ah here's another had some films developed two days ago.'

Rob looked at the two receipts. 'We have not seen any new photos, and it was just one film thirty-six exposures. Best we have a hunt for them.'

They went through all the obvious places in the study, kitchen and bedroom but could not find them. They did find binoculars and a camera in their respective bags hanging behind the study door. There was no film in the camera.

'Strikes me someone has been looking for something here. Not the local police no reason they would suspect anything. Natural causes as far as they are concerned.'

'The handyman?' asked Hamilton.

'Possible, I think it would be a good idea to speak with him' said Rob.

'I'll find out where he lives.'

'Good, I don't think we will learn anymore here. Drop me into the town please Ian, I'm sure you have other work to do'

'How will you get back?'

'Local bus, do me good to get a feel for the place.'

In Almunecar Rob found the photography shop where Styles had had his film developed. It advertised in English 'films developed in two hours.' Showing them the receipt he asked if they kept negatives, but the answer was no. 'We process far too many senor to do that.'

He tried to find the garage but it must have been too far out of the town. A town he found like a building site of cranes and cement mixers, dominated by concrete apartment blocks and souvenir shops.

At a small seafront cafe he had a hot dog and a beer. Hair of the dog he told himself. He felt he had no real feel for Commander Styles or what on earth he had wanted. He mooched around Almunecar for an hour then caught the bus back along the coast to Nerja. At the supermarket he filled two carrier bags with provisions avoiding any booze.

Passing bungalow 79 in the village he slowed hoping he might see someone but there was no sign of life. The communal pool was busy with children.

Back in his own bungalow he packed his groceries away. Then lay on the bed and had a siesta. It was dark by the time he woke. He was not hungry but did himself some beans on toast. He switched on the TV but after ten minutes switched it off. He tried reading one of the dozen or so books in the bungalow a violent thriller with a half naked woman on the cover, but gave up after a few pages.

In bed he lay awake for a while. Thinking, he concluded he needed a routine to fill the time, he needed to be confident in his own ability to take the initiative, he needed the traditional military ideal of order. Strange he thought something like Styles had.

Rob was up at seven-thirty he went first thing straight to the large pool dressed in shorts. It was empty the water cool and bracing. He did twenty lengths. Back at the bungalow in the garden, he did thirty press ups, thirty sit ups and thirty star jumps he was breathless when he finished but knew in a few days it would come good. Showered he cooked himself a hearty breakfast. He started a list of things he needed swimming trunks, some decent books. Then the telephone rang. Rob had not even picked it up before to see if it worked.

'Yes' he said answering.

'Duncan, Ian here.'

'Morning Ian you're on the ball.'

'Styles's handyman is a Brit, Roy Greaves and he lives in Nerja.'

'That's handy' said Rob 'give me his address?'

'He lives down in the town above the Brighton Cafe. He said he should be there most of the day just ask at the cafe. He sounded dead keen to speak with someone about Styles.'

'Have you any background on him?'

'Been over here about ten years shacked up with a Danish woman, builder by trade went bankrupt in the UK.'

'Right good' said Rob 'I will try and see him today.'

Chapter 5

'Yes I've been looking after the Commander's garden and odd jobs round the house as well, almost since I arrived' said Roy Greaves.

He was a short wiry man in his mid-forties, dressed in khaki paint stained shorts, and a threadbare faded blue short sleeved shirt. His bare toes poked beyond his sandals as if they were too small for him. He looked like he had not shaved for three days, grey and black stubble around his face. He looked nothing like a cafe owner more like a beach bum, bronzed by the sun his steel grey hair receding at the crown of his head but long at the back to his collar. The Brighton Cafe where they sat under an awning was spic and span. Greaves's girlfriend a good ten years younger than him, Tanya brought the coffee. She was a tall elegant blonde. She merely nodded toward Rob when Greaves introduced them. He pats her bottom, she doesn't like it Rob notices by the cold icy stare her blue eyes give Greaves.

'Well Roy anything you can tell me about the late Commander Styles?'

'Great fellow ideal customer, always paid on time with readies, I'll miss him.'

'Seemed a meticulous man to me' said Rob.

'Yes a place for everything and everything in its place. Ex-navy man he used to say it was from years living on ships.'

Except thought Rob he had not lived on a ship for years. 'Did he say much about his life take you into his confidence?'

'Not to start with it was strictly business but over the years bits and pieces.'

'Such as?' prompted Rob then taking a sip of his coffee which was excellent.

'He said he fell in love with Spain during the Civil War. Don't think his wife was so enamoured with the place, or that's the impression I got. So she buggered off back to the UK with the daughter. Now I have met the daughter, Linda, a couple of times when she came over to see her Dad, mind you never struck me as being overly fond of him.'

'How was Styles health wise?'

'That's the funny thing about it he was fitter than me, I've got a bit of a crook back, he didn't really need me other than he hated gardening.'

'So you don't buy this heart-attack business?'

'No way man, oh I know you can never tell, but if you ask me something fishy about the whole thing.'

'Did he mention anything he might have been doing over the last few days?' said Rob 'By the way nice coffee.'

'Hear that Tanya, Duncan likes your coffee' shouted Greaves, startling an elderly couple at one of the other tables, who promptly got up and left.

Rob saw the frown on Tanya's face; he wondered why she was entangled with someone like Roy Greaves, they seemed the proverbial odd couple.

'Well it was a bit odd last week. I called on him twice, did the usual garden clean up, but he had trouble with a tap had to get a new one for him. Went back a couple of days later to fit it, gave him a bell to let him know. Got there and he was out never done that before left a note and the key. That motor of his barely did ten miles a week. Yet that week he was out in it twice, if you ask me he must have met someone not just the usual shopping run.'

'How did you know he went out twice?'

'The first visit for the gardening he told me he had been to the supermarket. The second time I saw through the garage side window the car was gone.'

'Did he go out without the car much?' said Rob.

'Yes he was always out and about walking taking snaps of stuff.'

'Did he have many friends?'

'There were a couple of expats he used to play cards with in Almunecar. And once a month he used to go to the British Legion in Malaga, that's the only decent run the car got.'

'Nobody else?' said Rob.

'Check his address book, but I can't think of anybody.'

Rob let that pass, for he and Ian had been through the bungalow pretty thoroughly and found no address book. He made a mental note to check with the Spanish Police in case they had picked it up.

'Those photograph albums did he always keep them in such good order?'

'Hell yes, I had to build the shelves special for them, all had to be in the right order all dated.'

Except they were not when we got there thought Rob. 'But there was nothing missing' said Rob 'which would seem to rule out foul play.'

'Yes a right pickle' said Greaves with a furrowed brow he

35

shook his head slowly 'don't understand it Duncan.'

'Did he ever mention a Martin Judd?' said Rob.

'Judd, Judd no, I don't think so.'

'Well, you have been a great help' said Rob.

'What now?' said Greaves.

'Have to wait on the Spanish authorities for the autopsy.'

'You'll let me know about the funeral, like to pay my respects and all can't imagine there will be many there.'

'Yes we will keep you informed' said Rob getting to his feet, 'and once again thank you for your help and the coffee.'

Rob retraced his route out of the town along some narrow streets of the old quarter. He stopped at the Nerja Book Centre; he had noticed it on the way to the Brighton Cafe. A shop bursting with second hand books most in English, run by an expat. A quick look through and he had found four promising thrillers a Gardner and a Seymour amongst them.

'Best baker in the town' a female voice broke into his thoughts as he walked thinking about what Greaves had said confirming Styles's tidy nature, it meant someone had been there looking for photographs.

Caroline Gomez had come out of the bakers as he walked past. 'Hello' said Rob, she looked appealing in shorts and a T-shirt, 'I'll try and remember that certainly smells wonderful.'

'Tastes it too, heaps better than the supermarkets for bread, well, anything baked. Are you going back to the village Duncan mind if I tag along?'

'Be glad of the company' said Rob and they walked on

together. 'Dancing tonight?' asked Rob.

'Yes got a gig down at Fuengirola bit of a pain really means we won't be back much before two in the morning. Still they tip well. Are you busy Duncan?'

'Yes I have been looking at a property in Almunecar for a client' he wondered if he would ever get used to this lying and half truths. They crossed the road together into Capistrano village and all too soon for Rob reached number 79. 'What about a swim after lunch?' suggested Rob.

'How's about lunch first' said Caroline 'got a tuna salad ready enough for two, and not too heavy for the swimming.'

'Sounds wonderful' said Rob.

'Come on in then.'

Rob followed her along the short path to no 79. Inside the bungalow was well filled but clean. In the small lounge which the front door opened onto was a double sofa bed made up. One door led off to a bedroom which was open, the room was largely filled with another double bed neatly made as well.

'This is home to the four of us' said Caroline 'excuse the mess.'

Other than a clothes dryer full with interesting underwear, Rob found the place tidy.

Caroline opened the patio doors that led out into a small secluded garden ringed by bushes for privacy, there was a plastic table and chairs in the centre.

'We'll have it out there no room anywhere else' she smiled broadly, 'what will you drink? Only have soft drinks or beer I'm afraid'

'Beer will be fine' said Rob taking a place at the table.

'Won't be long' she called from the kitchen into which she had gone with the bags.

Rob watched her through the kitchen window. The Andalusia sun was strong and he was glad of the shade from the parasol.

'San Miguel' said Caroline returning with two cold glasses of beer she placed on the table. She disappeared again back to the kitchen; he could hear her singing softly but could not identify the song.

It struck Rob he had not taken much notice of her lost in his own world. She had the Spanish Moorish colouring albeit not as dark as the girls that had been with her last night, dark inky eyes that when they caught the light sparkled. Her features were finely chiselled like Lee Remick and she had similar waves in her dark hair a beauty like a vibrant flower. Yet her nature was more Anglo-Saxon, *fool* he thought *not Anglo-Saxon she's Welsh a Celt.*

'Here we are' said Caroline returning with a tray, she handed him a plate of tuna and a knife and fork, placed a bowl of salad in the middle with some serving spoons, the second plate of tuna she placed opposite Rob for herself. 'Now something's missing' she grinned 'stupid girl no bread. Always bread at a Spanish table my dada used to say.' She was quickly back with the French stick and some butter. 'Start Duncan don't wait on ceremony.'

Rob reached for the bread at the same time as Caroline their hands brushed.

'Oh' she said it felt like a mild charge of electricity, to her, it was something she had not felt before at such intensity. She looked direct into his brown eyes and knew he had felt the same.

'You first' said Rob.

'Thank you' she murmured and tore a hunk from the stick and then handed it to Rob.

Rob enjoyed the simple meal remaining largely silent as Caroline kept chatting away in her soft Welsh accent he guessed maybe she was nervous.

'I've been on the Flamenco circuit for three years now. It's beginning to tell on my legs suffered a few sprains and pulled muscles, lookey here' she said getting up. Moving clear of the table she stretched out each leg in turn, turning them from side to side so that he had a better view.

'They look fine to me' said Rob. 'But stomping your feet as you do is probably not good for them.' He could see that the right knee was slightly bigger than the left. 'Do the other girls that live here do the Flamenco circuit?'

'Concetta does, Maria and Carmen do maid service in the hotels, and they all come from the north of Spain. I do maid service sometimes if the bookings are down for a bit extra cash.'

Rob finished his lunch he noticed Caroline had a hearty appetite as well, he drained his beer.

'I'm embarrassed to say there is no more beer Duncan.'

'Don't be I have had enough thanks. Hope you don't think I'm a big drinker after last night, I got a bit lubricated.'

'No of course not, seen more drunks at the women's institute in Newport on a Saturday night than at a Flamenco show. Mind you some of the old men are right randy old buggers trying to grab you all over.' She picked up one of Rob's books from the table. 'I like a good thriller, do you read Chandler, just love Marlowe so hard boiled, yet funny as well.'

'Yes I like him' said Rob 'master of detective fiction great on description as well.'

Her eyes lit up 'That's right.'

'The first time I laid eyes on Terry Lennox he was drunk in a Rolls Royce Silver Wraith outside the terrace of The Dancers' said Rob.

'Wow, whooped Caroline 'great that's easy, opening line of The Long Good-Bye.'

Rob laughed nodding his head. He had read two volumes of the complete Chandler Collection on the Canberra heading south for the Falklands just four years before.

'What about' said Caroline consumed by a fit of the giggles composing herself she went on; 'The moonlight lay like a white sheet on the front lawn except under the deodar where there was the thick darkness of black velvet.'

'I remember this one' said Rob 'had to look up deodar, cedar tree with dropping branches.'

'Yes, yes' she said 'so did I.'

'Hmm' continued Rob 'that's not an opening line.'

Caroline grinned at him. 'Need a clue?'

'No just hold your horses' said Rob 'right I'll plump for The High Window.'

'Yes brilliant' clapped Caroline 'how long have you been reading them Duncan.'

'Re-read most of them in eighty-two we were heading for the Falklands on the Canberra.'

'You were a soldier?'

'No Royal Marine Commando with 42 Commando. Been out about four years now.'

'In the thick of it down there?'

'Something like that' said Rob. He began to wonder

perhaps he had inadvertently opened up to her too much. *Why can't I trust people?* He thought. 'How about that swim Caroline I'm beginning to boil here.'

'Right with you' said Caroline skipping away 'I'll get into my cossie.' She was back in a couple of minutes wearing a one piece white costume with a short black skirt over the lower half. 'Will this do?' she said.

'I should think so' said Rob 'you look stunning' her breasts looked firm and pert under the tight material, he tried not to stare.

They walked close together up the slight hill toward Rob's bungalow at the top of the village. Passing by the communal pool where there were only two people swimming. Rob began to think how much easier it would be if he could lose himself here in Andalusia Flamenco dancing with Caroline. In the bungalow Rob changed into his swimming trunks and grabbed a towel. They spent over an hour in the pool Caroline swimming in a white cap.

'It doesn't pay to get chlorine in my hair' she told Rob as they took a rest at the side of the pool.

'No it must be a job keeping it as good as you do.'

'Not really just a good shampoo and avoid chemicals.'

The white bathing cap made her face more rounded and just as beautiful. As they sat on the bottom of the pool Rob reached out instinctively for her hand under the water and held it. The tremor was still there he had felt as their hands had touched at the table. Somehow he had doubted it but it was there. And she did not resist in any way.

'Duncan' said Caroline 'did you feel something when our hands touched at the table?'

'Yes and now it's still there.'

He turned to her and kissed her lips softly.

41

They swam a few more lengths, but then some boisterous teenagers arrived having water fights and throwing each other in the pool.

'Shall we call it a day Duncan?' said Caroline.

'Yes I think they are a bit too energetic for us.' Rob noticed the boys watching Caroline as she got out, she had an elegant bearing about her some might call it pride but Rob knew better. They towelled off, both of them did not want the afternoon to end. Caroline removed her bathing cap and shook her hair free.

'Would you like a drink Caroline?'

'I'll tell you what I would like, a cup of tea.'

'Whatever you want.'

They walked back to Rob's bungalow. It was natural they held hands. Inside Rob asked. 'Would you like a shower Caroline, while I put the kettle on?'

'No I'll do that you go first.'

Rob set the shower on cool because of the heat of the day and got in. He reached for the soap and the door opened. 'Can I come in?' said Caroline standing there naked.

Rob reached for her and helped her in. He took her in his arms they both trembled with the kiss. Then they soaped each other's bodies, laughing when one or the other dropped the soap.

On the bed laying on towels to soak up the excess water they made love and slept afterward. It was only a few minutes then the phone began to ring.

'Hell sorry Caroline I'd better answer it, just stay there.' Rob hurried to the phone and snatched it up. 'Yes 'he barked into the receiver.

'Is that you Duncan?' said Ian Hamilton, sounding startled.

'Yes Ian what is it?' said Rob in a softer tone.

'Ah right, yes London want you to go back right away. I've booked you on the four fifty p.m. flight to Gatwick, you should be able to make it.'

'You're kidding, what do they want?' said Rob glancing at his watch which read three fifteen.

'No idea old man they don't confide in us. Ours not to reason why etc, but they did say to keep your bungalow on so they expect you to come back. You can pick the tickets up at the BA flight desk.'

'OK, ok I'll be on my way soon.' Rob replaced the receiver. 'Sorry Caroline, got to go back to the office in London right away some flap going on.'

'What, oh no' she said 'mind you your job is important not like dancing for a bunch of tourists.'

'Flamenco dancing has its merits believe me, art for one thing' said Rob sitting on the bed.

'Are you coming back?' said Caroline.

Was there concern in her voice thought Rob? 'Yes of course you can bet on that, and I'm to keep the place on so will be back but not sure when, sorry about the barbecue.'

'I will be waiting for you' said Caroline. She reached up and drew him down to her.

When Rob showed her to the door she reached up and kissed him gently and said. 'Don't be too long.'

There was a lump in Rob's throat when he closed the door. He was amazed the effect she had had on him. He had wanted to tell her the truth who he was, and what he did, but there was no time. Angrily he packed a holdall, checked he had his wallet and passport in the name of Duncan Forbes Dixon and was gone ten minutes later.

Chapter 6

9 September P.M.

By ten that night Rob Nicolson was paying the taxi driver who had brought him to Gower Street WC1 and the MI5 HQ. The Gatwick Express train had been crowded to Victoria with families returning from their two weeks on the Costas. Rob had stood all the way but he was glad of that after the flight sat in *cattle class* as he called it. He had managed to get the taxi easily at Victoria not wanting to take a bus or the underground.

He felt irritable and dirty as he took the lift up to Lanyon's office on the third floor. The duty officer had told him the Major was waiting for him. He was surprised to see how many of the offices were still occupied at that time of night.

'Hello Rob' said Julie Keyes brightly as he entered the office 'good flight?'

'No it was not, I thought I was supposed to keep my head down, keep a low profile. Instead I'm going backward and forward to Spain advertising the fact. And what was I told, use regional airports not the main ones?'

Julie's intercom buzzed interrupting Rob's tirade. 'Is that Nicolson?' came the clipped tones of Lanyon's voice.

'Yes Major he's just arrived.'

'About time too, send him right in.'

Julie raised her eyes to Rob there was an air of sympathy

about them as she nodded her head toward Lanyon's office door.

'Ah! Nicolson take a pew' said Lanyon as Rob entered the office.

He was stood by the window dressed in his usual blue pin striped suit, trousers immaculate, crisp white shirt even at this time of the day, Rob wondered if he had a supply of them hanging somewhere, still wearing the Guards tie. The only possible sacrifice to time was no waistcoat, or maybe today it was just a two piece suit. Rob slumped into the chair opposite Lanyon's desk and said nothing.

Lanyon drew the curtains. 'What do you think of this Commander Styles business?' he said walking briskly to his desk and sitting down.

'Hard to say I was not there long enough to reach any conclusion' Rob made a conscious effort not to say 'sir.'

'Yes unfortunate Nicolson but there are reasons we had to call you back.'

'I would like to know what they are Major.'

'All in good time, you must have some thoughts on Styles?'

'Well yes, there were two odd things. One, he was a meticulous man keen photographer yet his albums were all out of order, a small thing. And he took a roll of film of something just before he died, had them developed and they have disappeared.'

'Significant?' interrupted Lanyon.

'Maybe, I'm not sure. Anyway the second, he did not use his car much, perhaps once a week shopping only short runs. Yet two days in a row just before he died he did two longer runs even filled up with juice. We don't know where he went or why. I did speak to his handyman, Roy Greaves, and he had no explanation either. Of course we are still waiting on the Spanish Authorities but there's something odd about it.'

'Well Nicolson I can tell you about the missing photographs. Styles sent them to his daughter with instructions to send them to us which she did. We've had them blown up, switch out the lights behind you and come over here.'

Lanyon got up and moved to a small table where a projector was set up pointing toward a screen back against the wall. He switched on the projector and pressed the hand held switch. The first photograph was in black and white. Perhaps fifty naval officers lined up against the background of a ship's turret with two huge guns.'

'This is the Hood around 1936-37' said Lanyon. 'The officers sitting at the front are the senior ones' using a ruler he pointed at one in the middle 'Captain Arthur Pridham the Hood's Captain 1936-1938. And back here in the second row Styles and beside him Judd both Lieutenants at the time.'

Lanyon clicked the button again now there was a single officer in whites smiling into the camera taken somewhere on the ship's deck. 'Martin Judd, Barcelona April 1938 Styles has written on the back. Apparently Judd was killed in an air raid on the city on 8th April trying to rescue people from a burning building that collapsed on him he got mentioned posthumously in dispatches.'

The next picture was in colour taken from a distance with a telephoto lens in profile at a slight angle slightly blurred. It was an elderly man with a stoop walking toward a house in bright sunshine.

'Who do you think he is?' said Lanyon.

'No real idea, although looks vaguely familiar, would say by the style of the house has to have been taken in Spain.'

Lanyon brought up the next picture of Judd again in whites and the picture of the old man both smaller but side by side. 'I could not tell either but experts have taken a look and say these are one and the same person.'

Rob moved closer. 'Yes Major I think there is something about the face.'

'The colour picture is from the roll Styles had developed in Almunecar' said Lanyon.

'So Judd did not die in the air raid on Barcelona, so what has he been doing for what fifty odd years?'

'We have no idea, but take a look at this.' Lanyon moved onto the next picture. It was a large bulbous man, much bigger than Judd they were talking together outside the same house or the big man was talking Judd had his head slightly bowed as if listening intently. 'We know who the big man is. Krivitsky Boris, KGB up to a few years ago pretty high up then appears to have dropped off the radar in recent years.' He moved onto the next picture, this appeared to be the back of the house, Judd was moving away up a short flight of steps from the garden to the house, a slim blonde woman was beside him much younger than him. Two men were stood in the garden holding drinks talking together. 'The tall one is Vladimir Mirkin, known as the "Fox" the shorter one said to be a nasty piece of work Ruban Okudzhava. Intelligence on these two says they are Russian Mafia gangsters. We have a conundrum, what is a high ranking KGB man, two gangsters and Martin Judd a

Royal Navy deserter who has resurfaced after fifty years have in common? Switch the lights on please.' Lanyon switched off the projector.

Returning to his desk Lanyon picked up a large manila envelope and handed it to Rob. 'Here are the original photographs take a look.'

Rob went through them slowly. 'Do we know who the women are?' There were two both blonde and stunning, one the taller he thought about thirty, the other younger, maybe much younger even late teens.'

'No we have nothing on them' said Lanyon.

Rob continued looking after several minutes he put down the last one which had shown the house up much better. There seemed to be a high chain-link fence around the property which looked remote. He stared at Lanyon then said 'surely this is a job for Six?'

'Yes you are right, but they are a bit stretched at the moment and as you have started on this they would like us to continue. Calling in favours as such, you scratch my back we do it as well.'

'Right, so what do I do?'

'That is the intriguing part, go back out there. Try to find this casa grande, looks a big place; find out what they are up to. And another job is to take Styles's daughter out there, she wants to go to the funeral.'

'What am I some hired mourner, do I have to hold her hand?' said Rob his voice rising.

'Yes you will support her, not only that you will drive her out there. She doesn't fly afraid of it, what do they call that?'

'Aviophobia Major, not another one' said Rob.

'Another one what? said Lanyon raising his eyebrows.

'Woman on the flight over there hated flying sat beside me I had to literally hold her hand. Her husband could not have cared less. Mind you she managed it with a couple of stiff drinks.'

'Well Linda Styles can't or will not whatever.'

'She can drive herself surely?'

'Sorry no to that one, doesn't drive. Come on Nicolson be a bit more chivalrous after all she has lost her father.'

'Well according to Roy Greaves the handyman they were not very close.'

'Look Nicolson you are going to do it. Take that flash car of yours you got out of the Director. You are booked on the Plymouth to Santander Ferry the Quiberon. She sails tomorrow afternoon at three forty five p.m. twenty hour crossing gets in about twelve fifteen. You can pick up Miss Styles on the way she lives in Exmouth, practically on route. Your lot have some facility down there I believe.'

Rob was glad to see that being given the car by the Director after the Liverpool job rankled with Lanyon, but then he had not been on the books as an MI5 man then. And he still tried to wind him up with service rivalry, *you'll get nowhere that way mate* thought Rob, who answered in his best toneless voice, 'The Commando Training Centre Major, CTCRM, or as it is known sometimes The University of Life.'

'Well there you are a trip down memory lane. Staff sergeant Peters is waiting in the garage with your car all ready to go. Julie has all the gubbins, tickets and stuff. Oh! I almost forgot we are sending Josette Taylor out there for backup.'

'Is she fully recovered?'

'Just about but use her sparingly, she will be on R and R as well like you.'

Rob laughed out loud. 'Hardly feels like it to me' and thought *that's another one I'll have to nurse maid.'*

'Come on Nicolson this should be simple for a man like you. Any questions? said Lanyon and waited for an answer his patience ebbing away.

'This Styles woman how much does she know? And what about the Spanish?'

'Well she has seen the photographs of course. But I would not think they meant much to her. What her father told her in the letter that came with them we don't know other than he told her to send them to us.'

'Wonder why he did that, why not send them direct?'

'Apparently he was unsure of our location and in a hurry.'

'Why in a hurry?'

'Look Nicolson you will have to play it by ear. My advice try and keep her out of it. So on your way, I have a dinner party to catch up with' he said looking at his watch.

'Oh don't let me hold you up Major' said Rob sarcastically. 'Just one other point what about the Spanish?'

'Well use your loaf don't rub them up the wrong way now get going Nicolson.'

Rob got up and had his hand on the door handle.

'And Nicolson you would not be my choice for this but the Director seems to like you.'

'Thanks for your confidence Major it's you I have to thank for getting me into this outfit' said Rob opening the door and gently closing the door behind him. Although he really wanted to slam it but would not do so and allow *that bastard to think he was getting under his skin.*

Rob was glad to reach the altogether friendlier atmosphere of the garage. 'How's it going Nigel' he said greeting Staff Sergeant Peters when he entered the small office.

'Good Rob less than twelve months to retirement, I'm on the count down.'

Rob's eyes were drawn to the large calendar on the wall with the days crossed off; Miss July looked interesting draped over the bonnet of a Ford trying to wash it with her bulging wet T-shirt. 'You won't know what to do with yourself.'

'Don't bet on it lad. Your Jag's all ready to go checked her over myself changed the oil and filter love seeing fresh oil in an engine.'

'Great Nigel got a long way to go probably near a thousand miles and the same back.'

'Right you need to check the engine oil every day on long runs, the XK engines use a bit; I've put some cans in the back. Do you need a weapon, authorised to issue one?'

Rob considered this for a moment. 'No. Don't think so Nigel, can be more trouble than they are worth sometimes.'

'Up to you lad. Now remember check the oil and radiator every day, drive on your gauges.'

'I'll look after your baby' said Rob.

'Go on get out of here' grinned Nigel 'I want to get home to my Mrs.'

Chapter 7

At midnight Rob in the red E-type was on the M4 motorway heading south-west at a steady seventy. There was no great hurry and better to stick to the speed-limit he had decided. It would take him three maybe four hours driving to reach Exmouth. He would stop in one of the services grab a few hours sleep in the car. Have a bit of a clean-up, then breakfast which would then put him in Exmouth at a civilised time.

Near Bristol at the southern end of the Avonmouth Bridge he stopped at Gordano's services about one a.m. There were only a handful of cars in the car park. He relieved himself in the toilets, washed and brushed his teeth. Breakfast started at six, which left him about four hours to kill. He took a stroll around the car park. Got in the passenger seat and tried to sleep. The E-type did not have the creature comforts to aid sleep and over the four hours he managed about one, waking with cramp in his right leg. After that he dozed off and on.

A blue Ford Transit panel van came into the car park just before three a.m. It had a distinct burble to its exhaust note; the pipe instead of exiting to the rear came out the right side in front of the rear wheels and was a double pipe. Under the bonnet the Essex V4 engine had been replaced by a bored out V6 petrol turbo engine linked to a close ratio gearbox. Other not so noticeable modifications included light weight alloy doors and bonnet.

Two men sat in the cab, the shorter Frazer was behind the wheel, and he yawned then rubbed the stubble on his chin. 'It's the right reg' he said.

The man sat beside him was wiry he had a thin black moustache below a large hooked nose. He was Nosey Macintyre. 'Not many red E-types in this here car park' he snorted.

'And that's a fact' added Frazer.

'We could rub him out now no problem' said Nosey.

'Them's not the orders pal' said Frazer 'the council want to know what he's up to. Sounds like they lost track of him whatever he might have done. So we wait.'

Just before six Frazer observed the target get out of the E-type and stretch his body, feeling a degree of sympathy for his discomfort. There were many more cars in the car park now, pulling in to get breakfast. The target, wash bag in hand, headed toward the complex. Frazer waited until he had gone inside. Then gave Nosey a shove who was gently snoring. 'Wake up mate time for breakfast.'

They left the Transit and passing the E-type Frazer stopped and knelt down as if to tie a shoelace. He placed a bug, a small magnetic receiver about the size of a matchbox under the offside rear wing. They then went on into the cafeteria.

At a basin in the toilets Rob washed and shaved. Finished he grinned at himself in the mirror, thinking he washed up pretty good. Yet the last few years had taken their toll. His black hair was well flecked with grey. His hazel eyes looked tired. His face was lined, some might call them laughter lines, but most had come as a result of stress. Guilt lines might be more accurate. For Rob Nicolson had taken the lives of three people, all unavoidable, all very different. Not that he thought of them often, most of the time he kept them locked away in a recess deep within his memory, in a place he did not like to go very often. He winked at himself which seemed to restore some sparkle to his eyes.

When Rob entered the cafeteria it was already half full, he did not take much notice of those already eating breakfast, as he joined the small queue to get his own. He took his time over the breakfast which was surprisingly good even if the coffee was awful. It was seven thirty, he thought a slow run down to Exmouth should get him into the small Devon coastal town around ten thirty, a civilized time to pick up Linda Styles she lived at Merton Crescent on the sea front. It was fifteen years since he had been in the town, then in training at the Commando training centre a few miles inland on the banks of the Exe River. The town, a good run-ashore as far as he could remember.

After breakfast he took several turns around the car park to loosen up. He noticed the blue Ford Transit with the twin three inch exhaust pipes exiting from the side. *Must have something powerful under the bonnet* he thought *unless it was all for show.* But then nothing else seemed customized.

In the E-type he took a look at the map, the route was easy M5 to Exeter the turn off for Exmouth. He switched on the ignition pressed the starter button and the XK engine burst into life. He was on the motorway by eight cruising at sixty. In an hour he joined the A 376 for Exmouth he pulled in at the village of Topsham and found a telephone box, reflecting he would have to get one of those mobile phones, surprised the firm were not already using them. Linda Styles was pleased to hear from him. He introduced himself as Duncan Forbes Dixon told her he would be with her in an hour.

Back on the A 376 the road began to run beside the Exe estuary. Rob's mind ran back to the years of training and the gruelling demands of the Commando course. Six months he had spent there, running everywhere, mud marches on the banks of the river, crawling through the stuff, being forever wet through was a strong memory. Then the accommodation blocks came into view and the tower of the Death Slide leading onto the Tarzan Course.

Opposite the main gate of Lympstone Camp he pulled into the small car park for visitors. Rob glanced across the road to the main entrance and the marine sentry on guard, armed he noted L1A1, SLR, Self-Loading-Rifle, must be high state of alert he thought. The guard looked at him; he knew he was watching him. Wondering what he was doing just sitting there he would have already noted the registration number of the car. He might have already relayed it to the guardroom with his HT two-way radio. Rob got out the map and made a show of consulting it to reassure the sentry. He imagined him thinking *stupid civvy lost in his flash car; hope he's not going to come over here for directions what do they think we are, the AA?*

Rob sighed; his mind coming back to the here and now touched the starter button put a hand up to the sentry as he drove on, who just stared at the car retreating into the distance toward Exmouth. It was in the past, an achievement, thought Rob but something he would not want to do again.

It did not take him long to find No3 Merton Crescent in Exmouth just off the sea front. No 3 was a ground floor flat of three in a large house, one of a row of sprawling Edwardian Villas. He parked outside. Walking up to the front door he noticed the paint was flaking and cracked, as were the window frames, the net curtains looked threadbare and grey.

Rob knew little about Linda Styles, according to the brief file Julie had compiled on her she was twenty-nine, single worked for local government, not risen very high, her mother had died ten years ago. She saw little of her father just the odd visit, must have gone by train thought Rob *some journey that would be.* Yet Commander Styles had sent her the photographs to send onto the firm he must have had faith in her. He remembered Roy Greaves saying he did not think she was overly fond of her father, maybe he had been wrong.

There had been a brass knocker at the door, but only the striking plate was left and the number three had lost a screw and was hanging at an angle. So he rapped loudly on the door with his fist. There was no sign of movement so he did it again.

The door with a creaking wrenching sound opened a couple of inches. 'Damn thing' he heard from inside 'give it a shove please.'

'OK' said Rob 'stand back' and pushed it open with his shoulder it suddenly sprang clear the door having been swollen in the frame.

Entering he said, 'Duncan Forbes Dixon' extending his right hand. The woman before him was slightly flushed and dishevelled in a dressing gown belted at the waist giving the impression she had just got out of bed. Her blue eyes were penetrating she examined the offered hand that was hanging in mid air, then clutched the dressing gown closer to her throat.

'Oh! Yes I don't normally' she said nodding toward his hand.

'No matter' said Rob 'not always a good idea.'

'Can you close the door please, I don't usually use that one' she nervously giggled.

Rob had to put his shoulder to it again plus a couple of hefty kicks to get the bottom fully shut. 'You want to get someone to look at that door' he said.

'Yes I know but it is so expensive and who can you trust.' She led him inside he found the flat was untidy and dirty. Every cranny was crowded with dusty ornaments, china figurines, books piled up on the floors. It was like a vision from Dickens, he wondered if Linda was some sort of Estella. In what he took to be the dining room a space of large dimensions with a high once ornate ceiling where lumps of the intricate plaster design was missing. On the table was a large suitcase open with clothes strewn around on the chairs and the table. 'I'm just trying to decide what I need to take.'

'Right' said Rob 'how long do you intend staying in Spain?'

'That's just it I was hoping your people would have told me.'

'Well, Linda it's up to you. The Spanish Authorities the last I heard had not yet released the body. But I don't think it will be that much longer. And as to any will I don't know, do you?'

'Father did have a Spanish lawyer a Senor Howson in Malaga he holds the will. I have to see him, so much to do' she sighed.

'No matter' said Rob 'soon get you out there. The ferry sails this afternoon and gets into Santander about noon tomorrow, then maybe an eight to ten hour run.'

'Oh I hope it's not a rough crossing I could never stand that.'

'Weather forecast is good' said Rob 'light winds in the Bay of Biscay.'

'Here' she said 'moving a pile of clothes from a seat 'sit down Duncan please.'

'Rather assumed you would be ready to go' said Rob picking up a lacy bra between two fingers before taking the seat, 'not that we are short of time.'

Linda grabbed it from him giggling. 'It is such a job for us girls deciding what to take.'

'Well don't let me hold you up' said Rob.

It took the better part of an hour, after several re-packs to settle on the contents of her large suitcase. 'That's it done' she said trying to close the bulging case.

'Are you sure you need all this' said Rob having finally succeeded in closing the suitcase.

'Right my handbag is ready, get changed then I'm all yours.'

'You have the important things Linda, passport overnight bag for the ship?'

'Ah! Passport I knew there was something do I need an overnight bag?'

'You do have a passport?' said Rob.

'Of course I do' she said.

But by the set of her bewildered face, which reminded him of Judith Durham, Rob wondered.

'Now the question is where is it? I think in one of these' she pointed toward two built in cupboards either side of the fireplace chimney breast and started looking in the left hand one.

'Shall I have a look in the other one?' volunteered Rob.

'Please do' she said.

Opening the door a stacked pile of letters and old bills fell onto the floor. A brief sort through them revealed no passport. Next he started on a pile of Readers Digest magazines going back twenty odd years. Flicking through them he came across a passport used as a book mark. He opened it thankfully it was hers and still had over a year to run. 'Here we are' said Rob.

'Oh good' she said taking it from him. 'Shall I put it in the case?'

'No keep it in your hand bag' said Rob irritation clear in his voice.

'Sorry' said Linda 'I seem to have this affect on people all the time.'

'We do have a ship to catch, which will not wait' said Rob injecting calmness into his voice, while thinking *why me*. 'Right next an overnight bag nothing too big, just for your washing bag, maybe makeup, a change of underwear, night things.'

'Right' she looked nervously at the suitcase.

'Go and get a bag I'll open the case' Jesus, he thought *this is beyond the call of duty*.

She came back quickly with a large soft shoulder bag which was ideal to his relief. Taking a few things out of the suitcase and putting them in the overnight bag made it easier to close the case again.

'Right' said Rob 'you get dressed ready to go and I will put your case in the car.'

'Better if you go via the back door Duncan, the front...'

'OK no trouble' said Rob. Hefting the case through the back door and negotiating the overgrown garden, muttering 'bloody obstacle course' to the back gate that led out onto a side street. From there he lugged it around the block to the front where the E-type was parked. The case just fitted into the back of the E-type with his own holdall there was only inches of clearance to close the tail gate.

Retracing the route to the house to his surprise he found Linda dressed and ready to go. She was smart enough in a crisp white blouse, but the red mini skirt revealing a good pair of legs looked totally unsuitable for travelling. She had the large bag over her shoulder, a red fur lined coat over her arm and was clutching her hand bag.

'Good' said Rob 'all ready to go?'

'Yes I am' she beamed.

It was interesting for Rob watching her try to slide into the E-type passenger seat as he held the door, which gave him a good view of white knickers.

'Oh my' she said as she settled into the seat trying to pull the mini skirt down 'what a funny car. Damn' she cried as Rob slid in behind the wheel.

'What's-the-matter now?' said Rob.

'I haven't locked the flat.'

'Yes you have' barked Rob. 'You checked it three times and I switched off the water.'

*

By two thirty that afternoon the E-type was parked in row three of the queue in Millbay Docks Plymouth waiting to board the 12,000 ton Quiberon. Rob had gone into the ferry booking office to get their cabin details. He had not noticed a blue Transit Van join the back of the queue in row five. Returning to the E-type there was no sign of Linda. *Gone for a pee* he thought. The journey to Plymouth had passed largely in silence, no doubt because he had been abrupt with her. Not that it bothered him in the slightest.

A wisp of smoke was rising from the ship's funnel and boarding marshals wearing reflective yellow jackets had arrived checking the first row of vehicles. *Where the hell was she?* he thought. Then to his relief he saw her hurrying toward the car. She climbed in this time there was no flash of underwear as she had changed into trousers, which she must have got out of the case.

'We will be boarding shortly' said Rob. 'Our cabins are on deck four' he gave her the ticket to 401. 'The key should be in the door when you get there you give the ticket to the steward, I'm next door in 402.'

'Thank you' she said 'it looks so big the ferry.'

'Yes these ships carry everything you could want, restaurants, shops, cinemas, the lot.'

'I think I'll stay in my cabin if it's all the same to you.'

'No dinner tonight, it's on the firm?' said Rob.

'Don't think so' she said wrinkling her nose, she was already feeling queasy just looking at the ship. 'No I'll pass if you don't mind.'

'As you like.' He noticed the first row of vehicles begin to move off toward the boarding ramp. 'Won't be long now' he said putting the keys into the ignition.

Onboard with the E-type parked on the car deck, they made their way up to deck four, Rob found the cabins and without a word Linda disappeared into hers. Rob dropped off his gear, and made his way up to the lounge, he was gasping for a coffee having had nothing since breakfast.

Rob bought some biscuits to go with the coffee and took it to the seating area. He felt the old familiar tremble of the engines beneath his feet as the ship came to life *not long now* he thought. He sat in a deep armchair by the window with a good view of Millbay Docks. He could see the rooftops of Stonehouse Barracks not far away and reflected on just how many ships he had boarded at Plymouth, RN ships of the Old Grey Funnel Line. He had brought his Spanish road map with him to plot his route once they were ashore. He traced the route with his finger from Santander due south to Burgos about sixty miles mostly two lane road would be slow. Then motorway to Madrid about one hundred and fifty miles, another two hundred across central Spain Castile and La Mancha still motorway. Then through the Sierra Nevada Mountains to Granada and onto the Costa del Sol to Nerja another one hundred and fifty, six hundred odd miles in total.

It had been decided Linda would stay with him in the bungalow in Capistrano Village until she found her feet, a decision he was already regretting. It might have been an engrossing journey under different circumstances he thought. Instead it would be to get there ASAP. Still the route seemed simple enough Santander-Burgos-Madrid-Granada, Nerja.

Over the ship's tannoy system it was announced loading was complete and the bow doors closed. There was a slight shudder and the ship was moving. Rob folded his map drained his coffee thought about a second but instead made his way out on deck to watch the ship leave Plymouth Sound. Out past the breakwater the Quiberon edged gathering speed passing the Mount Edgcumbe Estate on the Cornwall side. He was easily able to pick out the house of Gweebarra as they turned south just to the left of the Victorian Fort Picklecombe from his position. The house where the traitor Allen-Cleary had met his end at the hand of Eve and as a result he had been recruited by MI5 as a freelance then, it seemed a life time ago but was only two years. It still hurt even now. *Better look to the future* he thought and turned away.

Back inside he wandered into the shopping area to pass some time, it was crowded with passengers. There to his surprise he spotted Linda at one of the check-outs. She had a pile of chocolate bars and crisps being rung up.

'You would be better off having a proper meal rather than that lot' he said coming up to her.

'Oh! Hello Duncan no this is better I can eat this in bed.'

The ship gave a slight lurch then riding a freak wave.

'There you told me it would be calm' said Linda grabbing hold of the counter with both hands.

The female shop assistant gave Rob a sympathetic smile. 'It could not be better Linda the car moves about more than this ship will.'

'No, no' she said gathering up the carrier bag and scurrying away back to her cabin.

'Shall I call you for breakfast' Rob called after her, but she did not turn or slacken her pace. 'I'll take that as a no' muttered Rob, but he had to admit she was looking pale.

'How will you be paying Sir?' said the shop assistant, 'pesetas or pounds?'

Rob laughed out loud; 'That was smart, well let's see better be pounds have to get some pesetas.'

In the forward bar Frazer and Nosey sat at a corner table they were on their second pints of Stella Lagers. Nosey drained his glass, 'another Seamus?'

'No, no more for you either need to keep our wits about us.'

'Why? Where the hell are they going to go, over the bloody side?'

Frazer considered that. 'Might be an idea, clean and all, but no, too much could go wrong, too many people about. No, better on the road we can choose our time and place, once we get the nod'

'What did they say about the woman? said Nosey.

'Likely one of them anyway collateral damage, not gonna lose any sleep over the bitch.'

Chapter 8

14 September

'Come on' said Rob impatiently drumming his fingers on the wood rimmed steering wheel. There were only three cars left and one of the car deck crew was walking toward him to investigate why he wasn't moving. Just then Linda appeared from one of the entrances leading onto the deck and hurried to the car. The crewman smiled putting his thumb up, Rob started the E-type.

'Sorry Duncan I forgot my handbag and had to go back for it.'

'OK you're here now' he said.

Off the ship they were stopped at the Spanish immigration/customs check point. Rob took their documents into the office, which received a cursory glance by a bored official, and a nod to be on their way. Back at the car he found another Spanish customs officer looking over the E-type.

He smiled at Rob; 'Magnifico vehicles senor, have a good trip' and saluted.

Leaving the dock area Rob eased the E-type out into the Santander traffic along the sea front following the 'all routes' signs. It was drizzling, a grey day. They were already an hour late.

'Are we going to stop for lunch Duncan?' said Linda.

'Why has your bag of goodies run out?' said Rob making

no attempt to hide the sarcasm in his voice.

The journey's bad start continued when Rob missed the Burgos exit, and found they were heading toward Bilbao. It began to rain heavier he doubled back to Vargas and got onto the Burgos road. But found the single carriageway road slowed them down as it was choked with slow moving trucks. There was only one stretch of dual carriageway of about ten miles where he could put his foot down.

On the Burgos ring road he stopped at some services at two thirty, it had a basic self-service cafeteria but with a good choice of food. To his surprise Linda started conversing in Spanish with the staff, she chose vegetarian paella along with a large chunk of cream cake. Rob settled on sausages from acorn fed pigs and French fries and a fruit salad. At the booth looking over the car park they ate in silence until finished.

'Your Spanish is good' said Rob 'you sounded pretty fluent?'

'I went to school in Spain for three years.'

'Right' said Rob 'but you were young when you left Spain?'

She nodded. 'I was ten when we went back to the UK. Never had much chance to use it since, but it has all stuck in my mind. Only takes a few minutes and I'm back with it. Mind you the regional dialects can be a bit problematic.'

'Good that could come in handy, if you have finished we have a long way to go 'said Rob.

'Toilet' she said 'five minutes.'

'Of course I need to pay a visit, and have to fill the car, I don't know how far it is to the next filling station.' Even though the car had been fitted with a larger eighteen gallon tank which gave it a range of some 350 miles over the standard 280. Recalling Nigel's advice Rob checked the engine oil then moved the E-type over to the pumps. Linda rejoined him there, she stood watching from the passenger side.

'How long before we get to the coast Duncan?'

'Hmm' he said replacing the pump nozzle and screwing on the filler cap, he looked at his watch, just after three. 'Would like to think we would get to Nerja around midnight.'

'Good' she said and opened the passenger door and got in.

Having paid for the fuel in the kiosk, returning to the E-type he noticed parked over in front of the cafeteria a blue Transit, he could not see the lower side another car obstructing his view but he could see enough to tell it was right hand drive. He walked on past the E-type until he could see the side there were the twin exhausts. *Well, well* he thought *I wonder how many Transits there are like that.* It had to be the same one he had seen on the M5, must have come across on the Quiberon same as they had. He had not seen it onboard *so* they *must have got off before us and we got lost yet they were behind us, just too many coincidences there.* Back in the E-type he noted down the number.

'Anything wrong?' said Linda glancing up from the map she had been looking at.

Rob was glad she was taking an interest. 'No just something I need to check on later, all systems go, next stop south of Madrid.'

He soon had the E-type cruising at eighty. The rain had stopped and the skies were clearing to a bright blue.

'What are your plans after the funeral Linda?' said Rob.

'Well I'm pretty sure Dad will have left the bungalow to me so there will be that to sort out.'

'What I have heard property sells quickly on the Costa del Sol. So you should not have much trouble selling it. If that's what you want?'

'That's the trouble, I don't know. There is not much for me in the UK. But I could never have lived with Dad. Now I have a choice I suppose Spain or the UK.'

You don't sound very enthusiastic thought Rob, but instead asked; 'Did you know much about your Dad's work?'

'Oh! That he was a spy, of course Mother told me, she said he had been obsessed by that world.'

'Is that why they broke up?'

'No I don't think so. It was something else, something in the past, mother was a jealous woman.'

'What an affair?' said Rob.

'In a way. She found out by accident he visited the grave of a woman, and she couldn't handle it competing with a ghost. Or that's what she told me but I was not all that interested at the time. I was just happy that the rows stopped.'

'Um, do you know who she was, the ghost, I take it you mean she was buried in Spain?' She did not answer. Rob glanced across at her she was curled up to the left, her breathing easy. Sound asleep. Rob smiled he eased his foot down further bringing the E-type up to ninety. Put some distance between us and that Transit. Get Ian to check out that reg number first thing tomorrow. *Have to keep a lookout for the local fuzz* he thought *don't want a speeding ticket.*

Half an hour later he heard Linda yawn and wake up. 'Nice sleep?' he said easing back on the throttle to the legal seventy-five.

'Yes thank you I didn't get much on the ferry.'

'Really' said Rob who had slept like a baby.

Linda began looking at the map again.

'Are you looking for something?' said Rob the rustling beginning to irritate him.

'Yes there they are up ahead, oh! It's so real he's so good.'

'Who is?' said Rob.

'Then one day I noticed a long low cloud lifting slowly above the southern horizon, a purple haze above the quivering plain-the first sign of the approaching Sierras. Laurie Lee' she said. 'Dad got me reading him.'

'Ah right' said Rob 'As I walked out one Midsummer's Morning maybe?'

'That's it Duncan, and if I'm not mistaken that is the Guadarramas up ahead.'

The road for miles had been, imperceptibly at first, climbing through fields of waving wheat and on into hills covered with pine trees.

'You're a bit of a romantic' said Rob.

'Where Spain is concerned I'm in love with the idea of the place, if that's being romantic you are right.'

It was after five when Rob pulled into the services a few miles south of Madrid. He refuelled the E-type taking his time; there was no sign of the Transit. *Maybe I'm being paranoid* he thought could they have followed him from London? No doubt Gower St was watched. Was it a mistake to take the E-type so easily recognisable? But

Lanyon had said to use his own car, was he being set up again? After all he was not his favourite agent. Yet it was the Major who got him into the firm in the first place. He was beginning to get the feeling he was being manipulated again.

There was no cafeteria here just a shop and toilets. Climbing back into the car he found Linda on board eating a chocolate filled croissant from a packet she had bought. Rob was amazed by her appetite.

'Would you like one Duncan?' she said offering the packet.

'No thanks' he said pressing the starter button. The next stop would be before they started to cross the Sierra Nevada Mountains to Granada and on to the Mediterranean coast.

Thirty miles behind them, keeping the distance consistent, was the Transit Nosey was driving. In Santander, Frazer had phoned a number in London and received orders to stop the E-type reaching the Costa del Sol.

'Looks like they have stopped up ahead' said Frazer reading the tracking monitor. 'We had better do the same and refuel.'

'Where do you reckon the Brits be heading?' said Nosey.

'According to the Bosses the coast which will be good for us, across the mountains there might be an opportunity. Then again he might keep going to Cordoba deeper south. Best close up to about ten miles.'

Nosey increased speed to ninety the van feeling stable although he knew much above that the feel from the steering began to get vague.

'Keep a look out for the Rozzers don't want to get

stopped' said Frazer 'need to get the guns out soon.'

After they had re-fuelled Frazer resumed driving, while Nosey took the M16 Armalite from its oil cloth sleeve the weapon had been hidden in a compartment under the floor. It had a folding stock, he checked the magazine, 350 rounds of 5.65, he knew it was ready he had loaded it. He unwrapped two hand guns from their oil cloth covering .44 Colt Magnums, and loaded them. *Jesus more than enough to take care of this man and girl* he thought. 'Down to about fifteen miles' he said placing the weapons back in their compartment.

'Ideal' said Frazer 'we'll close right up if he takes the Granada road.'

Around Madrid Rob had dropped his speed to the legal seventy-five there was more traffic about and he had seen two Policia Nacional cars. It was another two hours a hundred and fifty miles to the Granada exit. It would mean crossing the highest points of the Sierra Nevada at night but the road should be good going, not a motorway but lots of stretches of dual carriageway. He was in a good rhythm and was enjoying the drive. They were making good time and there was no sign of the Transit. Thirty miles south of Madrid Rob eased the speed back up to ninety. The sun was getting lower on the horizon and the road was edging around to the south west which meant he had to use the sun visor. Just after seven he turned off onto the Granada road turning south, ten miles later he pulled into services with a cafeteria.

'Lovely' said Linda waking up and stretching, 'I'm starving.'

Rob found that hard to believe, she hardly seemed to stop eating other than when she was asleep, the evidence was on the floor of the car with all the various food wrappers that were littered on the passenger side. Yet she was hardly fat *must have a bloody fast metabolism* thought Rob.

'We'll overtake them now' said Frazer, the Transit was only five miles behind. 'Catch'em coming from the other direction that'll give you a good shot that way.'

'Great' said Nosey 'they're as good as dead.'

They passed the E-type parked at the services and were beyond Jaen, climbing before the target began to move again.

'Here this will do' said Frazer a few minutes later it was a straight stretch climbing uphill ending in a sharp left hand bend, there was a track leading off barely two hundred yards after the bend where they could turn and wait.

'They will be on the outside coming up having to slow for the bend they won't know what hit 'em' he chuckled. *And if this idiot misses I can ram them right over the edge.* It was not a sheer drop but a hundred feet into a gorge any vehicle would be bound to turn over.

There Frazer waited; while Nosey went down to the bend watching the road below which was quiet only one other vehicle passed him. At last he spotted the red E-type below and ran back to the Transit.

'They're about two miles away' he shouted getting into the van winding down the window.

'Good' said Frazer turning the key to start the engine it turned over but did not fire. 'Shit' he said turning the key again it did not start. He pumped the accelerator twice.

'Jesus you'll flood it doing that' said Nosey 'they'll be on us in a couple of minutes' he had the Armalite ready and cocked the lever on automatic fire.

'Shut your mouth' said Frazer turning the key again the engine burst into life. He slammed the gear lever into first and they shot down the track wheels spinning heading toward the bend, into second gear gathering speed. The timing by accident was as near perfect as it could have been to ambush the approaching car. However there were three factors they had ignored or not noticed. One was the van's slow starting which made Frazer hurry. Two, the setting sun already touching the western horizon, it had been screened by clouds when Nosey ran back but now had broken through and momentarily it blinded them and they had not noticed coming up that the lane going down which they were in now was, from the fallen debris of steep craggy outcrops, partly covered in loose gravel from the rocks that had fallen onto the road.

Rob was in fourth gear the E-type climbing steadily around fifty coming up to the sharp left hand bend he slowed and changed into third, he was thinking he would have to put the lights on soon. He was glad the sun was now behind him as he listened to Linda gently snoring.

When suddenly the blue Transit emerged around the corner already beginning to slide sideways, he could see the figure at the window of the right hand drive van, a rifle in his hand.

Instinctive reaction took over there was only one choice, he stamped on the accelerator the E-type leapt forward while he twisted the wheel to the right away from the oncoming van but toward the edge of the road. Frazer blinded by the sun did not see the gravel on which the van lost traction beginning to skid sideways toward the other side of the road. Just when the van began to slide with a lurch Nosey pressed the trigger of the Armalite, the barrel was jerked upward and the burst of ten rounds largely went high only three hit the tail of the E-type as it sped by. Frazer trying to stop the slide put on opposite lock on the speeding van. This threw Nosey back into the van his finger still on the trigger got jammed and the gun fired another burst, shattering the windscreen, one round hitting the roof was deflected and smashed Frazer's left hand he cried out in agony and let go of the steering wheel while his foot slipped off the brake. The van straightened up and the Transit hurtled like an arrow over the side of the road rolling over three times like a cartwheel before coming to rest.

Rob sensing the van had missed them flung the steering wheel in the opposite direction keeping his foot hard down and the E-type missed the edge by inches. He watched the Transit in the rear view mirror go over the edge. Stopping the E-type gently it took him a few moments before he could let go of the steering wheel. He had to stop his hands shaking before applying the handbrake. Rob got out his legs and arms were still trembling, but he walked back down the road until he had a good view into the gorge. The Transit lay a hundred feet below on its roof there was no sign of movement.

'Amateurs' said Rob feeling relief at their lucky escape. He walked back to the E-type; he could smell petrol and the road surface below the car was marked by an increasing stain of fuel. Looking under the left rear he could see where the tank had been hit it was high up and was now only dripping. Three rounds had punctured the wing two must have buried themselves in the body the other was in the tank. Their shooting had been wild having missed the passenger compartment by several feet. He did not dwell on what might have gone wrong whatever it was had saved their lives. He went around to the other side checking for damage. It was then he noticed the transmitter box about the size of a matchbox. 'Bastards' he said pulling it off and hurling it into the gorge.

He got back into the car switched on the ignition, the fuel gauge was already reading over half. It would not leak anymore especially once they used a bit more. *Take it easy should make it* he thought.

'Um' said Linda waking up 'have we stopped?' She had slept through the entire encounter which had probably been over in two minutes.

'Just needed a leak' said Rob, pressing the starter button 'go back to sleep.'

Rob's eyes were glued to the gauges for the next ten miles before he began to relax as they all registered the vital signs of oil and water were good and the fuel gauge remained steady.

Down in the gorge the Transit lay at an angle on its roof. Nosey had been flung out on the way down and broken his neck on an outcrop of rock. Frazer inside the wrecked van lay on the roof the crash had broken his left leg with a compound fracture, but that was not what killed him, he bled to death from his near severed left hand. 'Oh! Should have been more careful' he whispered. He tried to think why before his eyes rolled up into his head and he died.

Chapter 9

15 September A.M.

It was just after midnight when the E-type drew up outside Rob's bungalow in Capistrano Village Nerja. He was exhausted after eight hours driving coupled with the nervous tension knowing how close they had courted death. Linda had woken up for the last two hours and he was glad of her chatter, as his body craved sleep. The fuel gauge had been touching empty for the last five miles. But he did not want to stop again; the E-type was too easy to remember even by a sleepy garage attendant. He unlocked the bungalow and unloaded their gear. He told Linda to take the bedroom he would make up the sofa bed for himself.

While she was unpacking, Rob drove the E-type over the low kerbs behind the bungalow that marked out a small turning place into the garden. Being one of the last to be built the bungalow backed onto open ground. In the garden the red E-type would be largely shielded from view instead of acting like a homing beacon, and he would get a cover for it as well *tomorrow* and looking at his watch *or maybe even today.*

Back in the bungalow he knocked on the bedroom door, there was no reply. He eased the door open; Linda was already in bed fast asleep her large suitcase was on the floor, open with clothes strewn about. 'Make yourself at home why don't you' he whispered and gently closed the

77

door. Thinking *I could probably have slammed it and it would not wake her.*

He made up the sofa bed had a shower and drank a cold beer from the fridge in the hope it would help him sleep. It did not work though exhausted he lay awake until past three, thinking all the time how had he been targeted so easily? It had to be the Provos they would have no scruples killing an innocent woman as well. His thoughts went round in circles always coming back to Gower St. *Were they just waiting for me* he considered it did not seem possible.

The telephone was ringing insistently. Rob opened one eye the sun light was streaming into the room. He closed his eye hoping the phone would stop. But it would not and he could not retreat to the warm arms of sleep. He could not quite reach the telephone from the sofa bed, so he crawled out to it. Picking it up Rob said in a husky voice in need of a drink, 'Yes alright.'

'Hello Rob' said a familiar voice he could not place, and he tried to think *who would be calling him Rob out here.*

Then it clicked. 'Josette, is that you?'

'Who else' she said 'am I glad to hear your voice did you have trouble getting here?'

'Did I ever, how do you know?'

'No matter I'll explain later will be over in ten minutes, I'm just across the road in a hotel.'

'Good' said Rob 'bring some food with you.'

Twenty minutes later Rob was cooking eggs and bacon which Josette had brought with her, she was sat at the small kitchen table.

'It's Duncan Forbes Dixon' said Rob in a low voice 'that's the name they gave me for cover out here, what about you?'

'Susan West, not very original 'said Josette 'yours sounds better.'

'Ya, like some chinless wonder.'

Josette laughed at that, she liked Rob there was no hidden agenda with him and she had him to thank for her life.

The only after effects Rob could see from the stroke Josette had suffered on the last case, a result of being drugged and her core temperature dropping so low, was when she smiled her mouth was slightly lopsided. She had put on a bit of weight her angular face was not so thin, and her brown hair was shorter she looked better for it he thought. She was still a snappy dresser even though she was wearing shorts and a T-shirt they were immaculate and well pressed.

'What about the news on the trouble out here?' said Rob as he used a slice to turn the bacon.

'Spanish Police are asking about a van that went off the road to Granada, packed with arms, the automatic rifle had been fired two men dead.'

'The van was souped up I spotted it at Gordano's services on the M5, not that it clicked then, what a fool, must have been following me from London...' Rob stopped speaking he could hear Linda moving about. 'Breakfast almost ready sleepy head' he called out.

'Oh! Company' said Linda coming into the kitchen still in her pyjamas.

'Don't mind Sue' she's an old friend 'Sue this is Linda.'

Josette got up. 'Come sit here Linda I have already had breakfast.'

The phone started ringing. 'I'll get that' said Josette.

Rob served breakfast which Linda set about with gusto.

'Thought you were a vegetarian?' said Rob.

'Where bacon is concerned I'm a carnivore and this bacon is lovely.'

'That was Ian Hamilton from the consulate' said Josette coming back into the kitchen 'he's on his way.'

'Why not' said Rob 'the more the merrier.' *This is like a bloody hotel* he thought *so much for the low profile.*

Linda finished her breakfast with two rounds of toast and went off for her shower and to get dressed. Leaving Rob to his coffee, Josette joined him for a cup.

'I need a car cover for the Jag; I've parked it in the garden around the back. Otherwise it would be like a beacon saying here I am.'

'Should be able to get one easy, mind you I'm surprised you brought it out here.'

'Yep, I should have known better, like a red rag to a bull, but Lanyon approved it.'

'He did? I wonder why?'

'Any leads on the Russians?'

'Only been here twenty-four hours Rob nothing yet.'

'Where are you staying?'

'Nerja Club Hotel, just across the road.'

'I know it' said Rob 'had a few drinks there the other night watched the Flamenco show.'

'Pretty crowded with tourists not ideal but the best I could do at such short notice.'

'You could have stayed here but I have to put Linda up for a while. Will pass her onto Hamilton ASAP get her out of my hair before she eats me out of house and home.'

'Yes I noticed she has a good appetite.'

'He can deal with the funeral and help her with her father's Spanish lawyer, although she speaks good Spanish.'

Half an hour later Ian Hamilton breezed into the bungalow. He was clearly taken with Linda, who was back in a mini skirt and a strapless top. 'We are here at your disposal' he beamed at her. Putting on a more sober face he added, 'at this difficult time. What would you like to do first Miss Styles?'

'Well maybe....' she began.

'Hang on a minute' Rob interrupted. 'A private word Ian.'

'Ah! yes Duncan, business first.'

'Let's go outside' said Rob, he did not want him to see the E-type, so he steered him toward the front door. Outside he wished he had brought a hat with him the sun was already fierce. 'What is the news on Commander Styles's autopsy?'

'Natural causes.'

'I don't believe that' said Rob.

'Still surely better for Miss Styles with that verdict she can get on with the arrangements. You don't agree Duncan?'

'Not with the autopsy. Having seen the photographs the Commander sent back through Linda. He did stumble across something and then he's dead. We don't know why, so Miss West and I will look into it. Now Ian I want you to look after Linda.'

'Be my pleasure Duncan.'

'But first I need a hire car. Second a place for Linda to stay, it's no good her staying here.'

'Of course not old-boy, would not be proper.' Ian began moving toward the door.

Rob pulled him back by the arm. 'Hang on any news from London for me or Miss West?'

'Not when I left to come here.'

'What about the Spanish have they been asking about an accident on the Granada road?'

'Why yes we had a memo from CESID about a couple of bods in a stolen UK registered van but how....'

'Never mind that, who is asking?'

'CESID, Spanish military intelligence old-man, not good.'

'Right we need to get in touch with London on a secure line, we'd better go to the consulate, but sort that car out first then we can pick it up on route.'

A short while later all four of them came out of the bungalow and started getting into Ian's Fiat 131. Rob was last locking the bungalow. Turning he saw Caroline coming up the road toward him she smiled and raised her hand in greeting. The smile left her face as she got closer and saw Linda and Josette in the car. Josette was in the front beside Ian, Linda in the back where Rob would join her.

'Sorry Duncan' said Caroline stopping. 'I'm obviously holding things up.'

'It's not what it seems' said Rob 'it's business.'

'Oh! Really you don't owe me anything, but business

with a skirt like that?' and she turned on her heel.

Rob felt the emotion in her voice, took a couple of strides after her, but knew it was not the right time or place, even though she had jumped to conclusions. He would have to put it right later. He got in the car and slammed the door.

'Trouble old man?'

'Just drive Ian' said Rob savagely.

Chapter 10

They picked up the hire car at Malaga airport a bog standard Seat 128, three-door hatchback. Rob drove it to the British Consulate following Ian's Fiat.

To say the Consul was not pleased to see them would have been an understatement. Davis Macmillan was a career diplomat who hated the *cloak and dagger brigade* who he felt *caused more trouble than they were worth.* But higher authority had deemed he was to facilitate them. Well so be it he would do the bare minimum. On the other hand he was full of sympathy for Miss Styles losing her father, and now having to deal with the Spanish and their labyrinthine laws, even if he questioned her dress sense, though he was impressed with her shapely legs.

'Mr Macmillan we need to use your secure line to contact MI5 right away' said Josette taking the lead as the senior agent.

'That is highly irregular Miss West' *bloody cheek this slip of a girl giving me orders* he thought.

'We need it now Consul, you can contact the Ambassador in Madrid if you need clearance.'

'That won't be necessary' he said 'the communications room is down the corridor to the left I will let them know you are on your way.'

'Good' said Josette 'we also need to meet with the Spanish Intelligence Service.'

'Well I don't know...' began Macmillan.

'I believe they have a Malaga office' interrupted Josette, becoming irritated by this Colonel Blimp character.

'Yes of course.'

'Right then get us an appointment with one of their people.'

'Damn cheek' he said to the empty room after they had gone. He flicked on the intercom to his secretary. 'Sandra arrange a meeting with the local CESID chap.'

'When for sir?'

'Right away damn it' he barked.

The telephone call to MI5 was not all that productive. Josette talked to Julie, Lanyon was unavailable. They had nothing much on the Transit other than the Spanish had recovered two bodies with Southern Irish passports; however contact with the Garda had established they were forged. The van registration number was from a vehicle stolen in Manchester six months earlier. They had no up-to-date information on any Provo's operating in Spain, and no further information on the Russians, MI6 had nothing either.

'The Major has marked it low priority. It looks like just an internal Russian thing. But we would like to know what Martin Judd has been up to for the past fifty years?'

'We feel it requires us contacting the Spanish CESID as they may have a different view.'

'Yes, right that will be OK, it really is their pigeon, just don't spend too much time on it that's the view here. You are both out there to rest and recover, so take advantage of it.'

Josette put down the telephone, the red light on the control panel went out automatically unlocking the heavy steel door of the secure room.

'They don't seem interested' said Rob who had listened into the conversation. 'Mind you Julie Keyes is good, and she's not overly fond of the Major either.'

'Who is?' said Josette 'so it's down to us.'

'Miss West' said a young woman waiting outside as they emerged from the communications room. 'I'm Sandra, Mr Macmillan's secretary; Captain Hernandez of CESID will pick you and Mr Dixon up in ten minutes outside.'

'Does he not want to come inside the Consulate then?' said Rob.

'No they never do, but it is their country after all' said Sandra.

A black BMW 3-Series saloon pulled up outside the modern brick built British Consul building at Moro Pareto dead on time. The passenger electric window lowered with a barely perceptible hum. The driver lent across, 'Senorita West, and Senor Dixon, I am Captain Ferdinand Hernandez you wish to speak with me, please to get in?'

Josette got in the front Rob in the back. The BMW shot away from the curb.

'I take you to a small cafe on the sea front, secluded we will not be disturbed.' Hernandez's English was immaculate if the tones were clipped. He drove in a wild style largely one handed, the BMW was automatic. This had his passengers hanging onto whatever they could. He shouted at other drivers, and wove through the traffic disobeying the rules of the road. They were relieved to arrive eight minutes later at the cafe close to the bull ring. They sat under an awning with a cool breeze coming off the sparkling sea. There were few people about. Hernandez ordered the coffees, the waiter clearly knew him.

'Si, that is the formalities now what can I do for you?'

'We have both been sent out here for rest, from MI5' said Josette. 'Perhaps you'd better explain to the Captain Duncan as you got here first.'

Hernandez sat impassive; he appeared bored slumped in his seat picking his very white teeth with a tooth pick, watching people walking by.

'Yes that's right I was sent out here mainly for R and R.'

'Excusy' said Hernandez 'what is this R and R?'

'Rest and relaxation.'

'Si, good yes, rest and relaxation a holiday, please continue.'

'I was also asked to check on Commander Styles he was a former MI5 man, retired but he had been insistent to see someone from the firm, the Consulate sent someone to see him but they found him rather belligerent.'

'What is Firm?' said Hernandez.

'The people who work in MI5 call it the Firm' said Josette.

Hernandez nodded and gestured for Rob to continue.

'By the time I got here Commander Styles was dead.'

The coffee arrived Hernandez spooned heaped sugar into his espresso then sipped it noisily, Josette and Rob had cappuccino.

'This is true' said Hernandez 'we knew of course of Commander Styles and his background. He served in your Six and something called NID.'

'Naval Intelligence Division, he served in that during the war, it no longer exists' said Rob.

'Gracious I have learned something' beamed Hernandez 'it is always good to learn something new every day. But the Commander died heart attack the doctora said neutral....'

'Natural causes' said Josette.

'This is right natural causes, forgive my English.'

'It is excellent Captain' said Josette 'let me show you some photos.' She took an envelope from her handbag selected one print and slid it across the table; it was of Martin Judd at the villa.

'Who is this?' said Hernandez picking it up.

'Martin Judd' said Rob who then told him the story of 1936.

'All interesting a deserter from your navy' and he shrugged his shoulders 'this may not be this Judd, it was a long time ago.'

'It has been confirmed by experts comparing photographs of him taken in 1936 and these that they are one and the same person.'

Josette slid the picture of Boris Krivitsky and Judd together, and then of Krivitsky, Mirkin and Okudzhava together.'

'Commander Styles took all these pictures Captain, they were developed at a shop in Almunecar, and a few hours later he is dead' said Rob. 'They are....'

'Krivitsky KGB' said Hernandez 'the other two Russian business men.'

'We would like to watch these people, if we could find out where this villa is' said Josette, sliding another clearer picture of the house across to the Captain.

Hernandez just glanced at it but did not pick it up. 'Given time we could locate that villa, but there is no need these Russians have moved. Ironically, is that the right word, I think so' he smiled. 'They are near Nerja not far from you I believe. What do you want to do?'

'We would like to watch them' said Josette. 'See if Judd is still there and try and find out what a naval deserter of fifty years, a high ranking KGB man and a couple of Russian gangsters are up to. Given that we think they killed Styles.'

'Our information is that Krivitsky is not so high in the KGB these days, the other two Russians, businessmen how they made their money is of no concern to us as long as they are clean here. After all my friends what does your press call us here, the Costa del Crime?' he chuckled at that. 'I like that Costa del Crime. But' he leaned forward closer to them and pointed at the photos scattered on the table, 'I grant you there is a mystery here and I don't like mysteries. So I propose we do a stake out as the Americans say, who loves ya baby' he did a passable imitation of Telly Savalas's Kojak. 'One of my men will accompany you and we only watch for twenty-four hours, longer is difficult for me. Yes' he said offering his hand to Josette 'is a deal?'

'Yes Captain it is a deal' said Josette taking his hand.

He turned to Rob offering his hand 'a deal senor Dixon?'

'Yes Captain' said Rob taking his hand 'a deal.'

'Good' he said 'call me Hernandez.'

Chapter 11

19 September

Two days later Linda moved out of the bungalow at Capistrano Village and Josette moved in. Linda said she was 'sad to leave Duncan' but it would be easier for her in Malaga close to her father's lawyers practice and the British Consul. And Ian had been kind enough to put her up in his flat in the town.

'I bet he was' said Rob to Josette 'he could hardly take his eyes off those legs' and they both burst out laughing. Yet it was better that she had moved on in more ways than one, they could both now work from the same base. That same day Hernandez telephoned it was all set for that night the 'stake out' and he was sending one of his best men, good with 'gismos.' In darkness they would move into an old ruin with a good view of the villa.

Marcus, swarthy, unkempt with a forty-eight hour growth around his chin arrived that evening around 9 p.m. in a large Volvo estate car. He had 'everything they would need', photographic equipment, food, utensils, and sleeping bags. They set out when darkness had set.

The tinkle of bells announced the approach of a large herd of goats. They were white, brown and black and some were a mixture of all three colours. They filled the road leading past the sprawling modern villa with its Islamic inspired

90

arches, towers and verandas, a couple of the goats stopped to tug at weeds growing between paving stones. Parked on the road that only led to the villa were two black Mercedes 500SE saloons and a white 380SL sports car. The goats sniffed at the cars but were not impressed by the Teutonic lumps of plastic and steel, as they presented nothing edible to these renowned consumers of plant life.

'Not for you mates' said Rob as he watched the goats and their goat herder through binoculars 'overrated if you ask me' he murmured about the Mercedes. It was the first sign of life they had seen around the villa since the stake out had begun. They had moved into the old ruined villa on top of a small hill a thousand metres from the target in darkness, the Volvo left half a mile away and they had carried all they needed into the position.

The ruined villa had lost most of its roof. It needed a huge amount of work, near rebuilding but bore its optimistic sign, in English 'For Sale or Rent.' *Rent that was a joke* thought Rob it must have been years since anybody had lived here. But now it was as if the whole Costa del Sol was for sale.

The target's occupants should be moving soon. Then they would find out just who was at the villa opposite. As if on cue a maid came out of a door leading to the servant's quarters, according to the floor map of the place Hernandez had supplied which looked like it had come from an estate agent. She carried a bucket, brush and long handled dustpan and started brushing up the red dust, carried in by the Sirocco Wind from North Africa, away from the pool area and patio. Another maid emerged from the same door with table cloths to lay up tables for breakfast.

'Here we go' murmured Rob, he lowered the binoculars and looked at his watch seven forty five a.m. the sun was already getting warm. In another hour it would be baking the barren landscape. He put the binoculars on the window ledge and moved back through an arch his feet crunching on stones and bits of dried out cement. Further back he passed through a doorway with no door where Josette and Marcus were asleep in their bags. *Green Slugs we called them in the mob* Rob remembered only thing was these were black.

Marcus was snoring and seemed to have a bad case of wind. Not a murmur came from Josette. He lit the small gas canister cooker and placed the kettle on it. He had to hand it to Marcus he seemed to have thought of everything. He then gave them both a gentle kick. 'Come on rise and shine.' He saw Josette begin to stir while Marcus's snore was uninterrupted.

'OK Rob I'm awake 'said Josette unzipping her bag she had slept in her jeans and black T-shirt.

He mouthed Duncan at her, clearly half asleep she had forgotten.

She nodded and smiled in acknowledgement.

Rob returned to the observation point picked up the binoculars and watched the two girls laying up the tables. They both had blue black hair tied tightly back and flashing eyes betraying their Moorish lineage. They were chatting away, not all that old he guessed in their teen's maybe. He switched on the receiver and picked up the head set he could hear their chatter clearly, the microphones were working well. Hernandez had done a good job to get them close enough to pick up sound on the outside at such short notice.

'Coffee Duncan' said Josette nudging his arm.

'Thanks' he said, he had to admit she was still good. He had heard no sound of her approach. He passed her the binoculars taking the steaming coffee mug.

'Well we should know soon just who is here' she said.

'Any bets?' said Rob.

'Other than a few Russians, we should be able to put their names to faces, but more important who else?'

'Manana' said Marcus arriving scratching his crotch 'set working OK?' he mumbled while eating a chocolate digestive biscuit.

'Works well just tested it' said Rob.

'But of course, one memento and I have the camera set up' said Marcus unzipping a large bag in the corner he took out a tripod and then the camera. 'Latest model this has piccolo computer, sees to everything.' He set it up at the second window well back so the sun could not reflect on the lens. He attached a large telephoto lens to the camera.

'Here we are' said Josette 'mine host Krivitsky.'

'I have him' said Marcus

'The Pied Piper' said Rob. He was dressed in white shorts and a T-shirt which showed off his muscled torso and powerful thighs his thick neck supporting his bald head. The two goons came out next and sat at a table with him, Hernandez's business men *not a chance* thought Rob. They set about their breakfast which seemed to consist of bread rolls and coffee.

'I take it that's his woman?' said Josette.

'Think so' said Rob using the binoculars Marcus had left while he was using the camera. Blonde, stunning her short skirt and blouse left little to the imagination. Then he broke into a cold sweat. 'Surely not' he murmured, there was no mistaking the tall walk of hers, extenuated by years of performing Flamenco. It was Caroline Gomez. There was another girl with her he thought possibly one of the girls who had performed with her at the Nerja Club but he could not be sure.

Josette had picked something in Rob's sudden intake of breath to alert her. 'Marcus can we pick up better what they are saying?'

He left the camera and picked up the headset and adjusted the receiver. 'Si they say about the area by the pool they talk in English' he handed the ear phones to Rob and returned to the camera.

Krivitsky had got up from the table and was talking with Caroline.

'What are they saying?' says Josette'

'Talking about money, for a show, a flamenco show, after a business meeting, missed that nothing now. They had moved further away. One of the others Mirkin has got up joined in, puts his arm around the Spanish girl's waist. Krivitsky shoves him away. He smirks at the girl but goes back to the table. Then they go back inside. A few minutes later Caroline and the Spanish girl leave in a battered Citroen.

The rest of the day passes with people coming and going. There is a bread delivery. The two Russian women use the swimming pool, and eat lunch under parasols beside the pool. Krivitsky joins them but they converse in Russian.

All the while the three watchers in the For Sale or Rent villa sweat unable to move far under the broiling sun, hats provide some shade. Everything is logged.

In the cool of the evening Martin Judd makes his first appearance. He is softly spoken the microphones barely able to pick him up when he speaks with Krivitsky who seems to defer to him. Is it the English man who is in charge thinks Rob? Why would a seventy odd year old be calling the tune with a KGB man? Who is this Judd, not in 1936, but now?

Mirkin and Okudzhava set out at dusk in one of the Mercedes saloons, but did not get far before running into the goat herd coming the other way, on the return journey to the hill side for the night where the herdsman has his hut. Honking the car's horn has no effect on the goats which brings the car to a halt as they flow around it. Passing by, the herdsman acknowledges them with a wave.

Krivitsky is clearly agitated by the noise they have made. Getting up from the table but Judd says something to him and he sits down again. Judd rests a friendly hand on his arm and talks to him to calm him down.

So you're a bit jumpy thinks Josette who is on watch while Rob and Marcus are packing away the gear in readiness for them to move out. *What have we learnt* she considers coming to the conclusion *bugger all.*

Marcus dropped off Josette and Rob at the entrance to Capistrano Village at midnight. They had made sure darkness was total before moving out of the hide at For Sale or Rent. The walk up the short hill to their bungalow through the estate passed in silence other than for the tune of the cicadas. Rob noticed the lights were out at No 79 maybe *a dance night* he thought.

'Do you want a drink Josette?' asked Rob once they were

back in the bungalow switching on the kitchen light.

'Love a cup of tea.'

'Tea coming right up.'

'That girl, the tall one talking to Krivitsky about a fee, she looked like that girl you briefly talked to before we went into Malaga and the Consul the other day?'

You don't miss much thought Rob. 'That is because it was her, Caroline Gomez, half Welch half Spanish, and she spends the season over here on the tourist trail with the Flamenco shows, which it looks like they are going to do one for the Russians.'

'Hmm' said Josette thinking, taking a drink of the tea Rob had poured. 'That's good tea. Do you think she might help us?'

'I do' said Rob 'but I don't know her that well it's just a feeling.'

'She seemed a bit put out the other day?'

'Yes when I left to go back and bring Linda out here we were just getting to know each other, well it was a bit more than that if I'm entirely honest. Then I come back with two chicks in tow makes me look like a right heel.'

'And one is Linda' smiles Josette. 'Yes I see, by the way what's happening with Dawn and you?'

'That's over; she could not handle me working for the Firm.' Dawn Jenkins had been Rob's girlfriend for four years but it had been a rocky relationship. 'Not that I had much choice but to come out here and lay low. Lanyon was up for her to come with me, but she would have nothing to do with the Firm. I managed to persuade her to go and stay with her Aunt on the South Coast.'

Still hurting thought Josette. 'Which means we have to

96

keep an eye on her?'

'Exactly, easier to cover us if we were both in the same place.'

'Regrets Rob?'

'She was a good girl, deserves better. Saved our bacon down in Cornwall with that Fowey River business. But I don't think, even without all the pressures, we would have made it.'

'Sorry Rob working for the Firm is not very compatible with affairs of the heart you need a strong person to take it. What about Caroline Gomez is she strong?

'I don't know but my hunch is yes, she's independent. I will have to see her and if we bring her in on this Judd business I want to be right up front with her. Tell her who and what we are?'

'Agreed' said Josette. 'Somehow I don't think Hernandez will want to do much more. We hardly found out anything we did not already know?'

'That's right, other than there is some big meeting coming up and what will Lanyon want?'

Josette drank the rest of her tea. 'I think we need to go on, something is happening out here, if we could get someone inside that villa we might learn what it is. We had better write up our report for Lanyon and send it off tomorrow, and also try and see Hernandez. But for now can I take the first shower?'

'Go on then' said Rob 'I don't know woman, taking over my space.' Yet Rob was far from happy he agreed they should try and find out what was happening. But no way was he about to put Caroline in danger if Josette was thinking about using her. They would have to find another way.

Chapter 12

20 September A.M.

It took Josette and Rob well over an hour to write up the report on the last twenty-four hours. They sat at the kitchen table, a scene of domestic simplicity. Josette in her dressing gown, a towel wound neatly around her head akin to a Sheik's turban, Rob in shorts and a T-shirt both glad to have washed away the grime of the day. Josette did the writing roughly at first, and then they discussed it before she wrote the final draft that they would send to London keeping it concise and to the point. It would be sent from the Consul's secure teleprinter exchange.

It was gone two before they went to bed, getting between the sheets of the sofa bed Rob wondered if he would sleep. Yet almost as soon as his head hit the pillows he fell into a deep sleep.

It was after eight a.m. that Josette shook him awake. 'Breakfast Rob, food' she teased 'what do you want?'

He lay there contemplating the choice. 'Toast, yes toast will be fine.' He then scrambled out of bed.

Over breakfast they decided Josette would take the Seat into Malaga to send in their report to London. And she would try to see Hernandez while Rob would see Caroline.

With Josette gone Rob hung around for a while, he tried to find the World Service on the Radio. But instead settled

98

on an English speaking Spanish Station all the news was bad the Soviet Nuclear Reactor in Chernobyl was in melt-down, but closer Basque Separatists had killed three people in Madrid in a bomb attack. He did not want to wake Caroline too early as she was likely to have had a late night. At nine he walked down to No 79, all the curtains were still drawn. He wanted to see her alone. He wrote a note in the pad he had brought with him for this purpose.

Caroline
Would like to see you ASAP it is important *did not knock as no doubt you were late back last night. I am at my bungalow all day.*
Duncan XX

He tore out the page folded it over twice and wrote Caroline on the outside, and put it through the letter box.

Back in his bungalow he had a drink of orange juice thinking they would have to get some more for tomorrow. Then he did some washing of his underwear. He hung it out in the back garden where there was a small line. He checked the car cover of the E-type and re-tightened two of the straps.

'What are you hiding under there?' said Caroline. 'Couldn't get an answer round the front thought you might be out here.'

She looked fresh to Rob given likely she had had little sleep. Her eyes were bright with no bags or blackness under them. She was dressed in all white shorts and a T-shirt, her long legs as he remembered brown and firm and their grip on him. In the sunshine her hair showed the highlights of its dark brown colour with its natural waves.

Rob loosened off a couple of straps and pulled back the cover off the bonnet of the car.

'E-type' impressive' said Caroline 'why the cover and what an odd place to park it?'

'Come inside and I will explain' he said replacing the cover and tightening the straps.

'What and join your Capistrano harem.'

Rob glanced up at her as he made a final adjustment to the cover and he was glad to see the smile on her face. 'I should be so lucky, come on' he said.

Inside he offered her a choice of drinks, she settled on water, he was glad of that and made the same choice. Caroline sat at the kitchen table nervously playing with her glass. Rob stood his back resting against the sink watching her.

'Come on then Duncan what is so important?'

'First my name is not Duncan Forbes Dixon. It is Robin Nicolson, most people call me Rob.'

'Well I didn't expect that, mind you might be better, need to get used to it Rob or Robin the liar, has got a ring about it. What are you some sort of spy?'

'No, I work for MI5.'

'Really you're joking,' she looked up at him 'no you're not, but aren't they spies?'

'MI5 is the security service, we tend to catch spies and implement the law. MI6 is the Secret Intelligence Service they spy on foreigners and generally work outside the UK.'

'Right' said Caroline sounding bemused.

Rob moved over to the table and sat down facing her, their knees almost touching. 'I was sent out here to lay low for a few months after a tricky operation in the UK. And I was given a new identity. It should have been just R and R, but a small job came up out here that I was detailed to look into.' Rob went on to tell her about Commander Styles and Linda Styles. 'Josette was sent out to give me a hand as things became more complex and she was on R and R as well, we had worked together on that same tricky operation on which she got badly abused.'

'Let me get this right, you Rob and Josette work for MI6....'

'No MI5' Rob corrected.

'Sorry MI5, and Linda is the daughter of the old agent that you think was bumped off after he recognised someone from fifty years back, hardly makes sense.'

'Yes that's right, but there is more to it than that. A group of men, Russians led by a KGB man Krivitsky and a Brit called Martin Judd we think killed Commander Styles and we want to know why, what had Styles stumbled across? We watched their villa yesterday not far from here.'

'Oh! I see now, I didn't like them I can tell you; you saw me with Concetta there yesterday. I thought we should have turned them down said we were booked up on that date Concetta didn't like them either. She said ask them for three times our usual rate to put them off. Which I did but they agreed just like that, paid a third up front in cash. And of course Fernando was delighted. We are down to give them a show in about ten days I think. You want someone on the inside to find out who attends and whatever it is they are up to?'

That was it thought Rob *but what do we want,* it was too much to ask Caroline to go snooping around. These people were ruthless and he would not put her in danger.

'Got it' said Caroline, beaming she touched Rob's hand on the table, there was still that tremor at her touch even if it was only to draw his attention to what she was about to say. 'You join our troop then you are into their place?'

'I don't think I would pass as a Flamenco dancer.'

'You let me be the judge of that. You were good the other night you would not be the *bailaor* the main male dancer. Nothing like that boy and even he's less important than the female dancers. Perhaps a hand clapper, we have ten days to rehearse, all you mostly do is just stand around with a smouldering look, a bit of foot work not too much.'

'What about Fernando, I take it he's the troop leader?'

'That's right but he will jump at the chance of having another man with us. Most Spanish men are not interested these days they want to watch football. Sometimes we have to perform without any men at all, which is far from ideal. It will be easy to get you in there, and then it's up to you.'

'Yes it might work. Will have to see what Josette says, she is the senior agent on this. She will be back soon' said Rob.

'Right what about a swim, that way we can start licking you into shape.'

'You're on then it's lunch on me.'

They were relaxed together, only once in the pool did Caroline slip up and call him Rob. There were only a few people in the pool hardly even within listening distance but it was better to point it out right away. He swam over to her taking her in his arms she put her arms round him drawing his chest onto her soft breasts. He whispered in her ear; 'careful with the names' then swam away. She was sorry he did. A long lunch followed the swim at one of Nerja's beach restaurants that specialised in paella.

Walking back into Capistrano Village nearing No 79 Rob's bungalow at the top came into view. The Seat was parked outside.

'I'd better see Josette on my own first' said Rob.

'Rob I hope we are not going to have secrets between us I know before I assumed things but....'

'No it's not that at all, but in our world it is often better not to know some things. It can be the more you know the bigger target you become. I'll come down and get you it won't take long.'

'How did it go?' said Rob finding Josette at the kitchen table with a cup of tea.

'Hi Rob. Took ages to get a response from London, guess what? They want us to keep an arms-length watch on the Russians just how the hell are we supposed to do that, bloody ridiculous?'

'Who did that come from?'

'I don't know, talked with Julie again.'

'That's odd' said Rob.

'You're telling me I sent the teletex in and it took them two hours to come back.'

'That means others have read it and instructed Julie to pass on the orders. What about Hernandez?'

'Not much there either would only speak with me on the phone, reading between the lines big flap going on in Madrid about the latest Basque Separatists attack. And now they are checking out Malaga with a big anti-terrorist deployment. He apologised but said the Russians were a

103

low priority, there was nothing he could do and suggested we drop it.'

'What's that, some sort of threat?'

'I don't think so, more a warning if we go on we are on our own. If we break the law we could be in trouble.'

'Hmm' said Rob 'what is your thinking Josette?'

She put two index fingers up to her temples and bent her head forward. For two minutes she said nothing. Then she lowered her hands and sat up straight. 'What do we know Rob? One, Styles was murdered agreed?'

'Absolutely.'

'Two, what motive did his murderers have?'

'That their presence here and in particular Judd's should not be revealed. But why then have a flamenco show and a party it's as if they are announcing their presence?'

'How come Judd as far as we can tell is in charge?' said Josette. 'And three, we need to find out what they are up to, but how? As to the show I think they are flamboyant people. They probably don't get much chance to party in the Motherland; on the other hand it may be just another smoke screen, having a party it says we have nothing to hide. After all that is pretty much what Hernandez thought.'

'Caroline has come up with an idea about that, after I confided in her as we agreed. That I should join the Flamenco troop and there would be no problem getting me into the villa. I don't think she would be willing to go snooping around on her own, and anyway I would not be happy putting her in that position.'

'Would you pass as part of the troop?'

'She thinks so, she will give me some lessons, and apparently men don't have such a prominent role in

Flamenco. And her boss is desperate for men to join the troop, at the moment there is only him and the guitar player. I would be just a hand clapper.'

'OK Rob so take me through it you go in with the troop what then?'

'The troop strut their stuff. I drift away when the audience is absorbed, might be best when they invite people to come up and have a go. I hide somewhere then have a look around when things are quiet. Maybe have a miniature camera, take pictures of the guests and anything else I can find.'

'Route out?'

There is that wall around the pool area about a six foot drop down to the lane where they park the cars, three ways out then.'

'I could be back-up at For Sale or Rent, oh, I don't know, I feel so tired.'

Hell thought Rob *she looks completely knackered only a few weeks from her stroke, is it too much for her?* 'Maybe....' he began.

'If you start the lessons it does not commit us and what about Caroline?'

'She is waiting down at No 79.'

'Good go and get her you were right not to bring her in before we discussed this.'

Josette and Caroline had an affinity almost from the start. 'You think this big old Marine has a chance of passing off as part of the Flamenco troop.'

'Oh! Yes he's a natural no problem and he won't have a major role.'

105

'The training or coaching' grinned Josette 'would need to be in private just the two of you somehow I think you might enjoy that.'

Caroline thought about that. 'Yes I know a place with a suitable floor, although I'm restricted on how much time I can devote to Rob given other commitments that I can't get out of. And Fernando given the time factor will expect Rob to join a show before the Russian job.'

Josette was impressed with Caroline's answer it was considered. 'Rob the other show means more exposure.'

'Where might this other show be?' said Rob.

'Either the Nerja Club, or Fuengirola another of our regulars, a hotel, most guests are older Brit's well lubricated most of the time.'

'Nerja might be too risky' said Josette 'can we ensure it is Fuengirola?'

'Yes I think so' said Caroline

'Right if we are all agreed' said Josette 'Rob starts training with you Caroline. Meanwhile we try and keep an eye on the Russians.'

'That's not going to be easy' said Rob.

'No it's not I will have to sleep on that one.'

'What are we going to call it?' said Caroline 'don't you people have codes for everything. What about Operation Flamenco?'

'Why not' said Josette 'whatever you like and now if you don't mind I'm going to have a sleep?'

'She looks tired out' said Caroline when Josette had gone to her bedroom.

'Yes I'm worried about her' said Rob 'she is damn good at her job, but only a few weeks ago she went through hell, almost killed her. We need to take care of her.'

Chapter 13

Flamenco Explained was not what Rob considered ideal bed time reading material. But Caroline had lent it to him and given their first session was tomorrow he thought he'd better give it a whirl, after all *she might ask questions.* Caroline had left mid-afternoon as the troop had a show in a hotel in Torremolinos.

Josette had woken in time for food. Rob prepared a corn beef hash, a staple of his Commando days, which she voiced enthusiasm for, though when they sat down to eat she just picked at the food. But the wine she gulped down made her talkative.

'You know Rob I have been in this job over twelve years now and what have I got to show for it? No' she raised a hand 'don't answer that I will tell you, bugger all.' She took another gulp of wine draining the glass. 'No family who want to know me, a pension the way things are going I will never see. You know I have escaped death four times, how many lives does a cat get, can't remember' she giggled and refilled her glass. 'But what could I do? Perhaps I could join Caroline's Flamenco troop? Except I have two left feet and no sense of rhythm, and I'm not glamorous enough anyway.' She gulped down half the glass, a few droplets dribbling down her chin.

'Cannot say I'm all that enamoured with the Firm' said Rob. 'But once you are in it how do you get out, look at Commander Styles even his past has come back to haunt him.'

'True, that's true' she said slurring her words.

'Maybe you should go to bed, you will feel much better with a good night's sleep' he said gently.

'You're right' she said getting up with her wine glass draining it, then picking up the half filled bottle of wine 'mind if I take this for a night cap?'

'Be my guest' he said.

Rob cleaned up the kitchen and did the dishes. He slowly opened the bedroom door, Josette lay fully clothed face down on the bed the wine bottle and glass lay on the ground empty. He could see her breathing she was in no danger so he picked up the glass and bottle and shut the door.

In bed propped up against pillows he started *Flamenco Explained* chapter one *Flamenco The soul of Andalusia.* *"Being the artistic expression of sorrows and joys."* He sighed, *gawd that's all I need more depression.* In the distance he could hear a party going on at another bungalow the sound of happy voices and the strains of *Spanish Eyes.* He went onto the next chapter *Flamenco Rhythm* reading on that; *"Rhythm is created by the guitar. But just as important is the beat created by hand-clapping and by the dancers feet in high heeled shoes."* And then there were castanets and *"graceful hand movements."* Rob tried to concentrate on the next chapter *Basic Steps* but fell asleep.

The sound of Josette in the shower woke Rob the next morning. She looked better at breakfast the dark rings around her green eyes not so pronounced. Her melancholy of the night before was gone like the wine, and her appetite was good, devouring three of Rob's beloved pork sausages from acorn fed pigs.

Josette checked with the Consul to see if anything had come through from London for them, there was nothing.

'That might be a blessing' he said.

'Yes, but they are going to bury Commander Styles at the English Cemetery in Malaga; they want one of us to attend.'

'Well there you are a nice outing....'

Josette shook her head. 'Afraid not, Miss Styles, Linda wants you to go. So you will have to fit it around your busy schedule.'

'Why me?' protested Rob.

'Seems to think you are jolly nice' laughed Josette 'so it is you and Ian.'

Caroline came at mid-morning for the first lesson, Rob taking the Seat drove west along the coast road. Directed by Caroline to Torre del Mar from there they cut inland for about a mile arriving at a farm. The place was deserted. Caroline had a key; she unlocked a large barn like building. Inside she led him into a large room with a laid wooden floor. In one corner was a set of drums on their stands, several guitars were hanging from the walls.

'Friends of mine own this place we have use of it for rehearsals' she said. 'Now then what size are you?'

'Sorry, size of what?'

'Feet man, lumps of meat, feet' she said pointing at a rack of shoes.

'Right, nine.'

'Let's see' she moved over to the rack 'take your shoes off. Looks like you will have to try them on to find a pair that fit. Most of these are handmade; they don't have the size marked on them.'

The men's shoes were like Chelsea boots with steel inserts on the bottom of the heels and the points; they were light but strong. Rob went through four pairs before he found the ones that were a reasonable fit.

'Good' she said, having already put on her own dancing shoes she had brought with her. They looked old fashioned, like something out of the 19th century, with a high square heel, a rounded toe and an over strap in the middle secured by a buckle. They looked odd with her shorts. 'Right then did you read the book yesterday?'

'Got through some of it, hardly up to a Mr Chandler yarn.'

'A bit boring I dare say. Now with all the stamping we do in Flamenco you need to keep your knees slightly bent then your legs act as shock absorbers, while keeping your frame upright not bending forward at the waist.' She adopted the pose. 'This will protect your back. Now keeping your toes on the floor move your heel up and down like this.' She demonstrated slowly, using alternative feet, and increasing the speed, the sound from the steel shod heels echoing around the room. 'This is one of the basic steps, go on have a go.'

Adopting the knees bent pose Rob found it awkward at first.

Caroline laughed out loud at his first efforts. 'No! No, no yes that's good' she encouraged. And for the better part of two hours she was relentless, putting him through four and twelve count foot combinations, moving onto the arms and wrists with long sweeping movements, while keeping the arms away from the sides of the body. Then reverting back to the feet exercises, making Rob balance on one foot, moving the heel of that foot up and down, then switching to the other foot, four repetitions on each and increasing the speed.

'OK' she said looking at her watch 'that's enough for today. Are those shoes good?'

'Not bad' said Rob he could not feel anything untoward.

'Take them with you, wear them a bit you need them to be comfortable.'

At the farm the next morning Caroline took Rob through what they had done the day before. After an hour she began to concentrate on the *Palmas,* the clapping. Showing him how to catch a pocket of air in the palm of one hand by cupping it and striking it with the fingers of the other hand, depending on the position of the fingers in the striking hand determined the volume achieved. And then how to follow the heel work of the dancers, with the clapping, and keeping time with the rhythm of the guitar, playing a CD of Flamenco music.

'You will have to skip the lesson tomorrow' said Josette when Rob and Caroline returned. 'Styles's funeral is at ten thirty tomorrow morning.' Caroline was not overly concerned at the loss of the session feeling her willing pupil was making good progress.

However that evening Caroline rang, Rob picked up the telephone. 'Hi Duncan' she said alerting him to the fact she must be in a public place. 'Fernando would like you to come to the show tomorrow night in Torremolinos just to meet you check on your progress. I told him your work restricts you during the day.'

'Right' said Rob hesitating wondering why she would say that. No doubt she had been put on the spot by her Boss. 'OK where is the show taking place, and what time?'

Josette was out in the garden on a lounger sunning herself in the cooler rays of the evening sun.

'That was Caroline, a problem, her Boss wants to meet me at the show in Torremolinos tomorrow night, and she told him I work during the day. I said yes.'

'Guess we have to go along with it' Josette removed her sun glasses 'it is a risk though.'

'The Russians are hardly likely to be there.'

'No, true' she said sitting up 'it is just me being overly cautious on the guard against needless exposure, and it is not only the Russians we need to be wary of. But we have to support her; you can go there after the funeral no point in coming all the way back here.'

Chapter 14

23 September A.M.

Rob and Josette were at breakfast the next morning when Caroline arrived, she had been worrying about what she had done and had not slept.

'I didn't know what to say when Fernando asked about you coming along. I could not say no given how important he thinks this Russian show is. He wants everything right. It's only the money he's worried about.'

'Not to worry' said Josette. 'Sit down have a cup of tea. Anything else we should know?'

'Well I said Duncan could not come to rehearsals during the day that would include everyone else, because he works at the British Consul, it was the first thing that came into my head. I'm not very good at this am I?' she said biting her lip.

'Nonsense' said Josette 'being put on the spot you reacted well and none of us saw that coming.'

'That's right' said Rob adding his reassurance. 'I'll drive down to Torremolinos after the funeral, take my gear with me.' Caroline had already got him the obligatory black silk shirt and black trousers.

It was another fine Andalusian day with the temperature rising when Rob arrived at the English Cemetery Malaga. He was already sweating in his dark blue light weight suit white shirt and black tie. He parked the Seat nearby, got out and walked to the cemetery entrance. Two wrought iron gates were open hung on large stone pillars that were topped by monumental prone British lions. In a few minutes the hearse drew up beside the gate that was not wide enough to allow vehicle access. The coffin draped in a White Ensign was unloaded by the bearers onto a trolley. By which time Linda and Ian arrived on foot from wherever they had parked. They greeted each other. Rob had to admit Linda looked stunning in black with a more sensible length of dress. The three of them followed behind the bearers as they pushed the trolley up a small slope into the cemetery. They stopped at the small Anglican Church of St George where they were met by the priest who exchanged a few words with them.

'If we are ready' said the priest.

'Yes' said Linda 'it is time.'

The priest murmured to the bearers 'Senores vamos.' And then in an unvarying tone began; 'I am the resurrection and the life, saith the Lord: he that believeth in me, though he were dead, yet shall he live, and whosoever liveth and believeth in me shall never die.'

Rob reflected as they moved deeper into the cemetery, the last time he had been in one he had shot a man dead. Soon they arrived at the open graveside.

Roy Greaves came hurrying up to the graveside. Even wearing a dark suit and black tie he still looked dishevelled. He nodded toward Rob, as if saying sorry I'm late.

'Man that is born of woman hath but a short time to live and is full of misery.'

Looking at the grave Rob noticed it was not very deep

and to one side lay a head stone that must have marked the spot and been moved for the interment. On it was written 'Tonya Antipov 1913-1941.' *Is this Linda's mother's ghost?* thought Rob. Given the shallow grave there must be another coffin in there. Or had he read somewhere to save space in cemeteries they sometimes doubled-up.

'Forasmuch as it hath pleased Almighty God of his great mercy to take unto himself the soul of our dear brother here departed, we therefore commit his body to the ground, earth to earth, ashes to ashes, dust to dust:' and the Priest droned onto the end. The remains of Commander Matthew Styles were lowered into the grave, and the four of them cast some earth upon the coffin. Linda spoke briefly with the Priest who then left in a rather undignified hurry. Soon the four of them were left standing alone at the graveside.

'Thank you for coming Duncan' said Linda.

'Everything else going OK?' said Rob, and then he introduced Greaves to Linda.

'Yes we have it all under control, Ian is being a great help' she said sliding her arm inside Ian's. 'Thank you for coming Mr Greaves.'

Rob pointed at the headstone; 'Is Tonya Antipov the ghost your Mother objected to?'

'I can't be sure but probably. Are you going to join us for lunch Duncan?'

'Alas no' said Rob thinking the funeral had not blunted her appetite. 'I have an appointment in Torremolinos' not revealing it was about eight hours away.

'Well' said Ian 'shall we say goodbye old man' he shook Rob's and Roy Greaves's hands and Linda kissed Rob on both cheeks, and then they walked away arm in arm toward the entrance.

'Any progress on who killed the Commander?' said Greaves once they were out of earshot.

'Not anything we could use as evidence, but we know he was onto something which we are investigating.' Rob added after a slight gap 'he was still serving his country' hoping it would make Greaves feel better.

'Still serving his country what a guy, well must dash' he said they shook hands and Greaves walked off toward the entrance.

Rob lingered a while he was in no great hurry. He felt a little guilty not going with Ian and Linda for lunch. He wandered around the cemetery, the grave of Mary Ann Plwes 1868-1911, marked by a large statue of an angel holding a cross was easily the most stunning sculpture. He went through the entrance into the old walled cemetery the oldest part. He removed his jacket he was getting hot and sat on a bench in the shade of some trees. It gave him time to think about all that had happened to him in a few short weeks. Not that it made that much sense. And he wondered about Caroline where was that leading. But he shut it away. He got up and made his way back to the entrance, as he reached it he had a good view to where Styles was laid to rest. Two men were at the grave he was sure one was Martin Judd. He ducked back into the entrance arch flattening himself against the wall, but he could still see them. There was no doubt it was Judd slightly stooped, the other one looked like Mirkin much taller. *What are they doing, gloating surely not?* he thought. He waited watching until they moved away. He followed making sure they left the cemetery, their progress fairly slow Judd walking with a stick. Rob then went back to Styles's grave. On the small headstone marked Tonya Antipov was a single red rose which had not been there before.

'Hello Marjorie I take it you must be English' said Rob, to the woman sat behind the desk in the gate house used as a visitors centre. Her name tag pinned to her blouse read Marjorie.

'Indeed I am, can I help you?'

'Yes I have just attended the funeral of Commander Styles in an official capacity. As a matter of interest I was wondering who Tonya Antipov was, I take it she is buried in the same plot?'

'Dear me the mysterious Tonya is popular today.'

'Oh really?' said Rob.

'An elderly gent asked about her only a few minutes ago, although he seemed to know she was here.'

'Yes I think I saw him leaving. Do you know anything about Tonya?'

'Nothing other than the Commander must have known her, he purchased the plot years ago, and I assume he had her buried there.'

'How interesting' said Rob.

'Also the Commander's lawyer recently contacted us in that under the terms of his will he has left a generous legacy with St Georges Church to maintain the plot, and his name is to be added to the headstone. Sounds frightfully romantic doesn't it.'

At a shopping area not far from the cemetery Rob found a public telephone booth. He rang the bungalow but there was no reply. At a nearby cafe he had an early light lunch, after which he tried his bungalow again still no reply.

Where the hell are you Josette, he had visions of her collapsed on the floor. She had looked far from well only twenty-four hours before. He looked at his watch now just after one, *nothing for it I'll have to drive over there.* It was an hours drive back to the bungalow in Capistrano Village he found it locked. Looking through the windows there was no sign of Josette. He tried No 79 but there was no answer there either. Back at his own bungalow he checked around the back, the E-type was hidden well under its cover the straps still tight. 'Where the hell are you Josette?' he muttered. He sat down on the lounger Josette had been using he had no choice but to wait. He wondered should he contact Ian Hamilton about Judd and the Styles grave, but it was likely he would not be at the office today.

'What are you doing here?' said Josette shaking Rob awake.

He yawned and stretched he had fallen asleep on the lounger. 'There you are I have been trying to ring you.'

'I took the local bus along the coast for a few stops looked around Almunecar, I'm getting bored out of my skull here. It was the spur of the moment, anyway what's up?'

'You sure it was Judd?' she said after Rob told her what had happened at the cemetery.

'Of course it was and the other one was Mirkin there is no mistaking him must be six foot six.'

'How did they know Styles was being buried?'

'Don't know' said Rob 'but it was not a secret. What about Linda could she be in danger?'

'I would not think so. I wonder who Tonya Antipov was and why Judd is so interested in her, we had better report this.'

Josette telephoned the Consul asking them to request from MI5 any information they had on Tonya Antipov and gave the dates on the grave stone. She also asked them to get hold of Hamilton and that he should give her a ring.

There was no news when Rob set off for Torremolinos at six thirty that evening; he needed to be there about eight to meet the troop, the performance starting at ten.

Chapter 15

Driving along the six mile seafront of Torremolinos for the second time Rob at last picked out the Pez Espada Hotel from all the others that all looked much the same. In the car park he noticed a battered old red Bedford CA minibus. Caroline had told him about the minibus they called it the cape, after the matadors red cape and a set of bulls horns were strapped to the bonnet.

The busy receptionist pointed Rob toward a corridor with a dismissive finger when he asked for the Flamenco troop. There were several doors leading off the corridor. 'Right which one' he muttered. He came to one which was ajar, he could hear voices inside. He poked his head around the door. There were several people in the room one was Caroline whose face lit up when she saw him.

'Hola Duncan, Fernando it is Duncan' she said.

'Sorry I'm late' Rob said striding confidently into the room although he felt anything but. 'Devil of a job to find it all these hotels look the same.'

Fernando Herrera was not what Rob had imagined a Flamenco troop leader to look like. He rather expected a tall thin man; instead he was greeted by a short rotund Friar Tuck look alike apart that is from the monk's garb.

'Si, si Duncan you are here all is good. Caroline por favor to introduce' he indicated the others with a sweep of his hand. At which they all advanced on Rob like a wave about to swamp him. Concetta and Tina he remembered from the

Nerja Club, both darker than Caroline smaller and younger, they looked like sisters but in fact were cousins. Isobel the lead female dancer the bailaora was older in her thirties. She looked a tough nut to Rob although her smile was friendly. Juan thin and small was the music man. With Rob now in the troop there were seven.

'Attention' said Fernando clapping his hands 'we begin soon.'

Rob noticed they all, apart from Juan who wore trainers, had their dancing shoes on, he put his bag in the corner with the others and changed into his dancing footwear.

'We begin Juan with sevillanas plenty of duende.'

'What's duende?' whispered Rob to Caroline.

'Magic spirit.'

'Flamenco recuerda, it is life, the air we breathe begin' said Fernando.

Isobel started alone just with Juan on the guitar to accompany her, she began with slow deliberate movements arching her body. As she began to speed up Fernando began singing in a harsh vibrating voice, the rest started clapping. Rob had no idea what to do so he joined in the clapping trying to match Isobel's steps. Then Fernando joined the dancing. The transformation in him was startling, Rob would not have believed it if he had not seen it with his own eyes, he seemed to grow six inches and lose twenty pounds the girls took over the singing.

Juan then switched to a small kettle drum and began a simple beat. Caroline took to the floor alone and started a dance full of passion her arms arched high her hands playing castanets. Fernando took up the singing it was as if he was tearing something from deep within him. Caroline worked up to a crescendo that left her lying on the floor at the end panting for breath. The two other girls then did a dance on their own that was much more light hearted with flashing eyes and suggestive poses. After which Isobel came back with a slower dance of intensity, accompanied by the guitar alone.

'Now for the touristas' smiled Fernando. Juan switched to a keyboard and began to play Spanish Eyes, and Fernando took up the song while Caroline, Concetta and Tina danced around him. They all moved seamlessly into Granada and onto Eviva Espana.

'Bravo, bravo' cried Fernando at the end, 'then we invite the audience to join us, all must do this Isobel?'

Isobel made a face in reply.

'Duncan you to help with the older ladies por favor. What about your voice a good baritone I think, yes you could sing one of the songs. You're English so much, much....' He struggled for the word.

'More articulate' suggested Caroline.

They have to be joking thought Rob with a sinking feeling in his stomach, who had never done any singing before other than the odd hymns and boozy nights out with the lads in the mob.

'Articulate si is right' smiled Fernando at Duncan.

'What about we do a duet with Spanish Eyes?' said Caroline

No, no please don't thinks Rob smiling at Caroline.

She takes Rob by the hand moving them into the centre of the room where she positions them standing facing each other. 'Juan the music please'

'Blue Spanish eyes' croaks Rob trying to follow Caroline's lead. Then his mind goes blank *what comes next?*

'Wait a minute' says Caroline, Juan stops playing. 'Don't worry about the words just la la it. Fernando what if we turn it into a dance between lovers?'

'Magnifico romantic is good.'

'Blue Spanish eyes' they began again Caroline moving around Rob, improvised it has elements of a tango. Rob feels like an idiot.

Fernando claps his hands, 'Gracias Caroline it needs work maybe for Fuengirola. Duncan such progress in two lessons. A short rest my people then change for the show.'

A glance at his watch told Rob it was nine twenty, the time had passed in a flash he felt exhausted. And there was still the show to come. To his chagrin everyone else seemed on a high. Caroline pulls him to one side away from the others and whispers in his ear. 'You are doing just fine.'

The show was nothing like Rob had anticipated. Performing in front of a live audience swept away his tiredness on a wave of adrenaline. He began to enjoy it, clapping away with gusto trying to look suitably intense and joining in the popular songs. The dancing with members of the audience reminded him of something akin to a scrum. The old girls he largely danced with were certainly game rather than trying to dance anything with a resemblance to Flamenco; it degenerated into a cross between the Gay Gordons and the Hokey Cokey. He did notice Caroline crush one man's toes with her heel as he became overly familiar with her bottom. After a few encores it was all over.

Rob was more than happy to give Caroline and Concetta a lift back to Nerja as it would save Fernando hours to drive there in his ancient van and back, as he lived in the village of Mijas not far from Fuengirola which was in the opposite direction. Fernando forced 4,000 pesetas on Rob, who tried to refuse until Caroline intervened. 'It's your pay stupid take it.'

'You were lethal with your heels in there' said Rob as they made their way out to the car.

'Ah! Yes you noticed, bums and boobs are not to be touched.' She took his arm to bring him closer and whispered. 'Of course there are exceptions to the rule.'

Concetta sat in the back of the Seat being the smallest; they pulled out of the car park of the Pez Espada just after midnight. They could still hear music coming from the hotel the DJ having taken over after their show. 'Some of them will still be going at three in the morning' said Caroline. 'Shall we have another lesson in the morning?' asked Caroline, as Rob took the ring road around Malaga.

'Should think so, although I need to see what Josette has planned.' He glanced in his rear view mirror; Concetta was curled up on the back seat asleep. 'We are waiting on some information from the Firm, so the chances are one of us may have to go to the Consul. Another thing about this duet?'

'You will be great, it just needs some work' she said confidently.

'OK, but not with the Russians, I don't want too much exposure there.'

'No of course not, I did not think about that, sorry. But Fernando with that show will concentrate on classical

Flamenco, the Russians will not get the average Brit tourist serving.' After that they were both silent for a while.

'Have you a family back home?' asked Caroline a few miles from Nerja.

'Mum and Dad, a younger sister.'

How do I get close to this man thought Caroline *he just reveals nothing.* Well not entirely she considered she knew he had been a Marine Commando. She decided to have a chat with Josette to find out what made him tick.

There was a long straight approaching the turn off for Capistrano Village, Rob noticed a black Mercedes pull out of the estate entrance. It turned toward them on the opposite carriageway heading toward Malaga or back into the town of Nerja. The street lights were good and he was able to read the number plate. He was sure the car was the same as one the Russians were using. What were they up to in the village? He was suddenly concerned for Josette, but said nothing.

Caroline was waking Concetta as he pulled up at No 79. Rob got out tipping his seat forward to let her out of the back.

'Gracias Duncan' said Concetta making her way up the path.

Reaching up Caroline kissed Rob on the cheek as he stood by the car. 'See you in the morning' she said.

'Yep I'll give you a shout' said Rob getting back into the car.

His vagueness felt like indifference to Caroline and her heart sank as she watched the car pull away.

Using the key he had taken with him Rob let himself into the bungalow he flicked on the lounge light. Everything to his relief looked normal. He gently opened the bedroom door.

'Hi Rob' said Josette from the darkness 'all alright?'

'Yes it went well.'

'Good see you in the morning.'

Again Rob found it difficult to sleep. What that Merc was doing in the village troubled him. Had they somehow rumbled them? It did not seem possible. And then there was Caroline, a fine girl, intelligent, she was making it clear she wanted more from him and he wanted more from her. But dare he risk it, people who got involved with him got hurt. He was not going to put her in danger, but had he already? Was she strong enough to cope?

Chapter 16

27 September A.M.

'A duet I had no idea you had such hidden talents' said Josette at the breakfast table the next morning, a broad grin spreading across her face.

'Yeh, ha, ha hardly keeping me in the background is it?'

'No, I suppose you could be so bad that they drop the idea?'

'That might get me dropped for the Russian's show. But Caroline reckons Fernando will not use the duet in that type of show.'

'Which is the important one.'

'What about that Merc sniffing around?' said Rob. The registration number as he had suspected had matched one of those they had logged in the notes of the stake out.

'I don't see how they would have anything on us. Might be something to do with the Flamenco show, or something we are in the dark about.'

'Yep' said Rob unconvinced 'think we should change the hire car just in case, we have both been driving that one for a while.'

'Good idea I'll look into it.'

With no reply from the Consul, Josette decided to go into Malaga to contact the firm direct. She dropped off Caroline and Rob at the farm on the way arranging to pick them up on her return.

The lesson started by Rob concentrating on his clapping role coordinating with the dancer. Caroline was professional as always, but her usual sparkle was lacking.

Rob was prompted to ask 'Anything wrong?'

'With me no, let's turn to Spanish Eyes.'

'Just one thing Caroline, let's not lose sight of the objective.'

'Yes I know that is your sole interest but you need to keep in with Fernando, so Spanish Eyes.' Then playing on a portable CD player Al Martino's version of Spanish Eyes, Caroline slowly built up a dance routine. Involving Rob being largely static, singing while she danced around him, the finish with her standing in front with her back toward him Rob's arms around her with her hands resting on his. Over and over they did it tweaking the steps to coordinate with the two and a half minutes of the song.

They did not hear Josette come in, the time flying past they were so engrossed. Rob had even made some suggestions. Until she said; 'Bravo, that's wonderful. What a voice, you could join the Firm's choir for carols.'

'That's what I keep telling him, he has a good voice, not much else but that can't be helped.'

'Awch' said Josette 'have I come in at the wrong time?'

'How did it go?' said Rob when he was alone with Josette back at the bungalow.

'Julie found out a bit of background for Tonya Antipov. Soviet agent during the Spanish Civil War, tried to infiltrate the Nationalist side, got caught. Was held prisoner in one of Franco's concentration camps, interrogated probably tortured, executed around 1939-1940. How her remains

129

ended up in Malaga who knows. Other than there was a camp at Ronda maybe Styles bought the body, bribed the guards. Anyway he bought that plot while he was with Naval Intelligence in Gibraltar 1941-1944.'

'So likely he knew her during the Civil War and perhaps Judd did as well.'

'Could have been the eternal triangle, two men in love with the same woman, which in some ways casts a shadow over Commander Styles.'

'Does it make much difference to what we are trying to do, which is what just remind me?' said Rob sarcastically.

'Don't lose sight of the aim Rob, who killed Styles and why. I think the why is far more important.'

'Did London have anything else to say?'

'No, nothing they did not even query why we wanted the Antipov background. On the other hand, I found these two beauties in the security office at the consul and borrowed them.' She took two miniature Minox EC cameras out of her handbag about three inches long and as wide as a matchbox. 'These are digital, take fifty pictures. Don't have to wind them on or anything just press the button, battery operated. Used one before, you can hide them in all sorts of places. Behind a shirt button, don't do it up like so' she demonstrated with her blouse' some tape to hold it in place. Just need to work out how to press the shutter button without making it obvious. And don't use the flash that gives the game away. Do you think you might persuade Caroline to use one?'

'Doubt it' said Rob 'I'm not her favourite person.'

'You are stupid sometimes Rob she's got the hots for you.'

'I don't know about that but if you let people get close in this job they get hurt.'

'And you don't want her hurt, admirable' Josette looked Rob right in the eye 'she's already in this, that was her decision and you might ask yourself why would she do that?'

That night Josette and Rob went to the ruin For Sale or Rent to watch the villa for a couple of hours. There was not a lot of activity both Mercedes saloons were there and the sports car. Boris Krivitsky came out for a smoke leaning on the wall that enclosed the pool area. He was briefly joined by Mirkin they exchanged a few words then both went back inside. Rob felt there should be no problem getting out by dropping down into the lane from the pool wall. Josette was not so sure other than the front door or the kitchen entrance it looked like the only way out. Most of the windows were either too small or were covered by wrought iron as was the Andalusia fashion.

'Come on in' called Josette from the kitchen when she heard Caroline knock at the door. The lesson today was in the afternoon, as Caroline had been helping out at the Nerja Club Hotel changing the beds for the turnaround of weekend guests.

'No pupil?' Caroline observed sitting at the table.

'No he's out the back fiddling with his car' said Josette who was stood at the sink washing lettuce for lunch.

'Oh! Good I wanted to talk to you about Rob, he's, he's', she hesitated 'so cold at times.'

Josette sighed and turned to look at Caroline 'what is it

with you two don't you talk? Cold, no I don't think so, he feels too much for our work it's not good that's his trouble. He is focussed on this job and worried sick about you.'

'Worried about me why?'

Josette put the lettuce in the serving bowl with some cut tomatoes and cucumber. 'There are Scotch Eggs as well, suitable food for dancing on?'

Caroline nodded.

'Rob has had a couple of tough cases recently. In the last one I worked on with him one of our fellow agents was killed, and a friend badly injured. He doesn't want to put you in danger. It was my idea to ask you to help get him into the Russians villa not his. These people we are dealing with are ruthless.'

'Yes I know about the Russians' Caroline frowned 'he was straight with me from the beginning, well almost, I want to help.'

'Great, but that does not make it any easier for Rob. But I'll tell you this he likes you a lot. If he didn't he would not....' Josette stopped, hearing Rob come in the patio door.

'Think I will get a couple of gallons for the Jag to.....Oh! hello Caroline' he said coming into the kitchen.'

'Hola Rob' said Caroline 'looking forward to our lesson?'

'Yes, yes I am' he said moving to the sink to wash his hands.

Good thought Caroline that is more positive.

'Caroline do you think you would be able to use one of these?' said Josette sitting at the table after they had finished lunch showing her the miniature camera.

'Maybe' she said examining the tiny camera. 'I could hide it in the folds of my Flamenco dress, I have it in my bag. We could try during the lesson Rob.'

'Yes do that' said Josette 'you would only be trying to photograph the audience.'

'That's right nothing else, and not at all if it's risky' added Rob.

'We know the Russians were on this estate yesterday, do you know any reason they might be Caroline?' said Josette.

'No, well I think the fat one liked the look of Concetta.'

'And you' said Rob.

'You mean Okudzhava, nasty piece of work nicknamed the 'burner' likes to brand people. So you stay clear of him' said Josette.

Parking the Seat at the farm Caroline reached for her door handle but Rob held her other arm. 'Wait a minute Caroline let's just talk for a while.'

She sat back in her seat and kept staring straight ahead waiting for him to speak.

'I like you a lot, I may seem preoccupied at times that's because I am, but when this is over I want to know you better.'

Caroline continued staring straight ahead. 'I like you too but I cannot turn my emotions on and off like you can. I know you cannot drop the ball. But that is how I am. Perhaps we should have gone slowly at the start?'

Rob could not see her face beyond her curtain of dark brown hair, he put a hand up gently to move it aside and at the touch she turned to face him, a single tear was moving down her left cheek. She leant forward and kissed him on the mouth, and was pleased to feel him respond and he squeezed her hand. 'I don't regret that at all' he said.

The lesson went better as both were more relaxed. Even Rob's singing in Spanish Eyes he felt was better. The camera proved awkward for Caroline to use, other than putting it in the top of her bra where it protruded.

'It might be better with a black bra, or what about lower down at my waist if I wore a belt of some sort?'

'No I don't think that would be much good maybe it's not such a good idea.'

Chapter 17

The Las Palmeras hotel the venue for the show was right on the seafront of Fuengirola, still an active fishing port backed by the Ochre Mountains. A favourite with the British package-holiday tourists, it was a place Fernando's troop performed in often. The routine followed the same that Rob had experienced at Torremolinos, with a rehearsal before the main show. All were pleased with the Spanish Eyes piece Caroline and Rob had worked up, and with the chemistry between them it had that extra dimension. One or two hiccups did not matter.

Yet it struck Rob almost as soon as the show started they were in trouble. When Caroline had done her solo Flamenco number after Isobel's opener, he noticed two men come into the large lounge with the stage at one end, they stayed back by the bar. One by his height was unmistakeable, the Fox Mirkin, the other probably Okudzhava. He knew by instinct they had not dropped in just for a drink they were watching the show intently.

Shit thought Rob *what were they after, how did they know we would be here?* It must have been through the troop. But there was no way out. No escape, he had to perform, blank them from his mind. Caroline had spotted them too; she gave Rob some nervous glances. But when toward the end she started Spanish Eyes she was superb, not missing a step or a word under the pressure and with her lead Rob rose to the occasion.

135

'Wow, wow Duncan, it's us.'

Rob's heart sank at the end taking their bows out at the front of the stage he spotted Beryl Hope in the audience.

'Duncan, Duncan it's me' she shouted his name.

He had to acknowledge her to stop her. One redeeming factor was she did not come on the stage to join in at the end. Horace was slumped at the table probably drunk thought Rob. He got off the stage as quickly as he could before any of the others.

'What do you think they are doing here?' said Caroline her face contorted with fear. She had come straight into the men's changing room to find Rob he was the only one there.

It was Rob's worst nightmare. 'There must be a simple explanation. And that damn woman shouting my name out, it was like a neon sign.'

'Who was....?' began Caroline. But Fernando came into the room.

'Ah! Caroline rapido, Duncan good, changed to meet our Russian clients, mucho dinero' he said rubbing his fingers together. 'Meet for the vino ven rapido Caroline' and he pushed her toward the door.

Rob was quickly out the door, he waited for Caroline who quickly came hurrying out of the women's changing room, in bare feet carrying her trainers. He had found a store room and led her into it. Putting his hand over her mouth he gently closed the door holding her close in the dark. 'Listen' he whispered into her hair. 'That idiot must have invited them here.' He took his hand away from her mouth.

'I think so Rob I knew nothing about it.'

'Has he done this before?'

'Yes he thinks we should entertain his clients, we don't like it and have told him so but money speaks to him. But you don't have to go.'

'What and leave you to it, I don't think so. You could come back with me?'

'Oh! No way Rob and leave Concetta and Tina to it, look you don't have to worry; we have dealt with the likes of them before.'

Rob was sure they would not have encountered anything like the Russian Mafia before, a few randy businessmen maybe. But he knew he should not get involved, given Beryl Hope had been shouting his name at the top of her voice. *What the hell should I do?* he thought.

'The objective comes first that's what you told me.' They could hear voices outside, no doubt Fernando was looking for them to join the party.

'I know but I'm not happy. But I trust you, phone me as soon as you can'

'Yes of course I will' she kissed him on the lips while he hugged her.

'Stay in here Rob I'll lead them away.' And with that she was gone.

Rob waited five minutes after which he made his way out of the hotel through the kitchens at the back. He drove out of the car park hating leaving, though he had no choice but to go back to Nerja now as that was where Caroline would contact him.

He drove the Seat too fast, as if driving flat out might dispel his feeling of self loathing at leaving Caroline in the lurch. *Bugger the mission* he thought but there was nothing he could do now. There was no news when he reached the bungalow; he was restless waiting for the phone to ring.

'Trust her Rob she knows what she is doing' said Josette, Rob's pacing about waiting for the phone to ring had woken her.

'Oh I trust her it's the others I don't.'

It was just after three a.m. the phone rang. Josette had gone back to bed. Rob snatched it up at the second ring, to his relief it was Caroline.

'Are you alright?'

'Yes of course we are.'

'I'll come and get you?'

'No you will not, get some sleep. We are in a hotel in Fuengirola, it was easy getting away. We often perform here the owner is a friend, he has let us have a room for the night free.' She told him the hotel and roughly where it was.

'I'll pick you up in the morning.'

'Yes can't wait to see you, now go to bed Rob.'

Chapter 18

30 September

Early the next morning Rob picked up the girls in Fuengirola. They told him amongst much giggling how they had given the Russians the slip. Once the Russians had got rid of Fernando and the others they moved with the girls to a nightclub. 'They drank gallons of vodka' said Caroline. 'The barmen soon got the message not to put much alcohol in our drinks. Then we went to the toilet and got away to our friend's hotel only a few streets away.

That probably won't put them in a good mood reflected Rob. After dropping Tina in Malaga and Concetta at Capistrano Village, Caroline stayed with him when he went to the garage to get some fuel for the E-type; she was keen to look over the car.

'Did they say anything about the meeting?' said Rob as he drove back to the village.

'Yes I think they said the Boss is coming, but most of the time they were speaking to each other in Russian.'

'Did they notice I was missing?'

'No they were certainly not interested in men.'

'Hi you two' said Josette when Rob and Caroline got back. 'Ian's been on the phone London has been in contact. They are sending someone else out to join us. He is arriving this afternoon we have to pick him up at the airport.'

'Who is it?' said Rob.

'Randall, Derek Randall, I have met him a couple of times supposed to be a Russian expert.'

'Good they are taking this seriously at last, but you don't seem impressed Josette' said Rob.

'Could be a fly in the ointment, Randall is MI6 and not the best, you wait and see.'

'Lanyon did say at the beginning we were doing six a favour, maybe why he has not been on our backs on this one.'

'Hmm, with only two days to go I don't like it, a distraction. Anyway he's coming and we have to put him up.'

'Well he's not bunking with me' said Rob.

'You can stay with us' said Caroline.

'I must say that has its attraction' said Rob grinning. 'But four women could be too much even for me.'

Caroline punched him playfully in the ribs. 'Carmen and Maria have the weekend off they are going home so we have a free bed.'

'Right that's the accommodation sorted' said Josette 'think somehow I have drawn the short straw with Mr Randall.'

In the garden Rob took the cover off the E-type, and raised the one-piece bonnet to check the oil and water as Caroline watched. 'Can you drive?' he asked her.

'Yes had a licence since I was seventeen haven't driven for a while, last time was the Cape when Fernando had to see his mother in Madrid and we had a show booked.'

'If you can drive that old Bedford I should think you

could drive most anything.' He showed her how to check the oil and fill the engine if required, the E-type took a quart of oil, and the coolant level was fine. Then he went onto the tyres. Caroline got down on her hands and knees to follow what he pointed out. After closing the bonnet he poured the fuel they had got from the garage into the tank, two gallons.

'These are the bullet holes' he explained not wanting to scare her but he felt she should know. 'Another one went through the tank high up, she has a long range tank eighteen gallons, but until I get it changed probably wise not to put more than fourteen in, any more would just leak out.'

Caroline examined the bullet holes putting her index finger into one. 'I can't feel anything inside' she said.

'No, gone further into the body probably have to strip out the interior around the back to find them. Come on get in the driver's seat you can start her up.'

Caroline slid into the seat and stroked the big three spoke wood rimmed steering wheel with her hands. 'Nice' she said.

Rob helped her move the seat forward. Then with the door still open he knelt on the ground beside her. 'Right first thing on cold start-up, the choke, that lever on the right, top of the dash' he pointed it out 'push it right up to the top.'

'Like that?' she said.

'That's right hold it there, now with your other hand switch on the ignition and wait, hear that ticking?'

She nodded.

'That's the fuel pump wait until it stops. Right it has stopped, press the starter button.' The engine burst into life

141

with a strong bark from the exhaust.

'Wow' said Caroline delight on her face.

'Blip your throttle a couple of times' Rob touched her right leg pressing on it 'that's it now bring the choke down to about half way.'

'About there?'

'Yes good now ease the throttle down bring the revs up to about 1500 RPM' he pointed at the rev counter 'just for a couple of minutes. Then you would move off shutting the choke right off in a mile or so. But as we are not going anywhere just shut off the choke now and let her tick over.'

'I can't see the end of the bonnet' she said raising her bottom 'must be awkward to drive.'

'No it's OK you soon get used to it. The steering is heavy at slow speeds but on the move no problem. If it wasn't for the situation I'd take you for a spin.'

'Would you let me drive?' Caroline smiled.

'Why not, if you feel confident, what car would friend Marlowe have driven?'

'Ah! Trying to catch me out' she giggled, Bogie in The Big Sleep had a Plymouth Deluxe I think in the books may have been a Lincoln Continental.'

At Malaga Airport that afternoon Rob was surprised when Derek Randall emerged from arrivals. He guessed he would not see fifty again, short and going bald, dressed in a tweed suit more apt for the Highlands of Scotland rather than the heat of Southern Spain. A pipe jutted from his mouth.

'Derek Randall' said Josette as they met him 'we have come to pick you up.'

'Right good; give me a hand with my clobber.'

142

Picking up the old brown suitcase held together with string that Derek had deposited on the ground Rob asked; 'Is this it?'
'You have it my boy let's go.'

None of them took any notice of a slight man of five foot six who had arrived on the same flight as Derek Randall, pass out of the airport exit pushing a trolley with two bags on it. His passport checked by the Spanish passport control was British and read Ray Lewis from Southampton. His accent was neutral some might put it somewhere in the Home Counties. His usual name however was Sean Rice. Not that that was his real name, rather adopted to sound more Irish, his trade that of hit-man assassin. He noticed the man and woman meeting the fat sweaty bloke from the flight. Two of them he recognised already, he had been well prepared. Outside a blue Ford Cortina was waiting for him. He climbed in beside the driver and lit a cigarette.

In the car Randall informed them he was starving. 'Bloody airline food swill, let's try some authentic Spanish fare.'
Rob was startled, not once did Randall ask for identification or even where they were going.
They took him to one of Nerja's sea food restaurants, where he devoured a large bowl of king prawns followed by a sword fish steak, washed down by a bottle of Penedes white wine. Josette and Rob just picked at some tapas dishes.
'No foreign dosh old fruit' declared Randall 'see to the bill,' which Rob did as Randall further advised 'give them a good tip'
At the bungalow Randall collapsed onto the sofa bed fully

dressed, not even taking off his shoes and was soon snoring loudly.

'Hmm' said Rob 'this is a top MI6 agent they are kidding.'

Josette grinned; 'Different isn't he?'

While Randall slept Rob took his gear down to No 79, the girls were out but Caroline had given him a key. He was glad to be alone he could think about tomorrow night without distraction. He practiced locating the camera inside his black silk shirt holding it in place with black masking tape. From under the dash of the E-type he had removed the commando dagger; he tried strapping it to his right leg. Given he would not be dancing at the villa it felt fine. He had also bought a pencil torch in the town which he felt might come in handy. Finished he took a swim in the pool which late in the afternoon was deserted, he did thirty lengths.

He found Caroline was back when he let himself into No 79 she was in the kitchen unpacking groceries.

'Are you with us for dinner Rob, I've got some steaks?'

'You bet' he said mustering as much enthusiasm as he could 'I don't think I could face another meal with the dustbin.'

'The dustbin?'

'Mr Derek Randall, boy can he eat, but I better check with Josette if there is any change of plan, grab a shower first.'

Rob was surprised to find Randall awake sitting at the kitchen table in shirt sleeves drinking tea, and consuming a plate of biscuits, when he walked in.

'Ah! Nicolson my boy, good, Miss Taylor was about to scoot down to get you for our o-group.'

'Cup of tea Rob?' said Josette.

'No thanks.'

'I think I could force another down Miss Taylor' said Randall.

With them all sat around the small table Josette looked from Derek to Rob *guess it is down to me to start* she thought. 'We believe Commander Styles was murdered by a Russian group meeting here on the Costa del Sol, what reason they had to kill him we don't know. Or what they are doing here.' She then related the story for the benefit of Derek. He did not interrupt other than for slurping his tea, which Josette found annoying. 'Our plan is for Rob to go into the Russians' Villa under cover as part of a Flamenco troop; he has had some lessons with Caroline who we have taken into our confidence. Once inside we hope he can find evidence of what they are up to, or who has come to the meeting.'

'How very John Buchan the Flamenco idea' sniggered Derek. 'Certainly original, but odd having a show at all.' He stopped speaking for a few minutes sucking his teeth.

Josette looked at Rob and shrugged her shoulders.

'Right' said Derek sitting more upright. 'Krivitsky Boris, KGB Colonel, born Leningrad 1941, during German siege of the city must have been difficult for his mother. The people were reduced to eating rats, even human flesh some reports said. Education State University of Leningrad then named after Andrei Zhdanov. Joined the GRU, Soviet Military Intelligence in 1968 from the Army, promoted to

Major five years later on fast-track to rise high in the organisation. In New York 1979 believed instrumental in obtaining FBI secrets, 1980 transferred to KGB Soviet Intelligence Service. Promoted Colonel 1981, ran a honeytrap against an MI5 agent to spy for KGB. Fall from grace, too hard-line for the Gorbachev regime, side lined.' Derek hardly stopped to breath. 'Mirkin Vladimir, the "Fox" born Kiev Ukraine 1950, joined the Soviet Army for National Service 1970, selected for Alfovtsy in 1973 trained Leningrad 401st special school of the KGB. Served in Afghanistan 1980-1984, believed to have become involved in Afghan drug trade, dropped out of sight.

'Okudzhava Ruban the "Burner", born Vladivostok 1952, little known. Served Soviet Special Forces Afghanistan 1981-1983 enjoyed torturing prisoners. Tried to kill superior officer, deserted. Resurfaced Odessa 1984 engaged in drugs and prostitution. Dropped out of sight.' Derek paused to lick his lips.

'Question, what does a passed over hard-line KGB Colonel and two Soviet Special Forces soldiers, now maybe Russian Mafia, have in common?' He looked at Josette then Rob.

'There are two women with them who seem to only speak Russian' said Rob.

Derek nodded: 'Have you any pictures?'

'Yes of course' said Josette 'we should have shown you them first.' She got the large envelope and emptied it onto the table.

Derek spread them out and picked up a picture of Martin Judd speaking to Krivitsky. 'Who is this?'

'Martin Judd the naval deserter who....' began Rob.

146

'This is' interrupted Derek 'Antipov Boris, KGB Colonel. Birth unknown served in Spain during the civil war advisor to Republican Intelligence. In World War II NKVD specialist in British Intelligence, believed to have run Kim Philby for a time. Stalin doubted his loyalty yet he survived the purges. Under Brezhnev he was promoted KGB Colonel, instrumental in the downfall of Yuri Andropov head of the KGB. He was looked on as a possible successor. Now it is obvious he was *oboroten* a shape shifter, a turncoat to his country never to be entirely trusted, an *inostranets* a foreigner to boot.'

Rob told him about the grave of Tonya Antipov. Also that Caroline had heard Mirkin and Okudzhava talk about the 'Boss' was yet to arrive.

'Yes there is more to these people. Any help from the locals?'

Josette told Derek about Hernandez and CESID.

'Sounds like we are on our own and we should assume by now the delegates to this meeting are already here. Better take a decko at this villa later on.'

'Yes I agree' said Josette 'but Rob had better settle down with Caroline for tomorrow. What time are you leaving Rob?'

'We are going over to the farm for rehearsal tomorrow afternoon. Fernando's going to pick us up about two. We need to be at the villa about eight the show is due for nine.'

'Have you everything you need Rob?' said Derek. 'Artillery etc?'

'No, I don't think it would be wise going in there with a gun, hard to hide it, have a knife but I'm not sure about that either?'

'I think Rob is right' said Josette 'he's going in for information not to start a fight.'

'OK, your party' said Derek 'let's hope you don't get caught with your trousers down and all you have in your hand is your dick' he sniggered.

'We also need to be alert to the Provo's sniffing around' said Josette, she related to Derek the attack on Rob on his road trip over.

'Right tomorrow we will get the latest profile on their activity in southern Spain, and any news on Russians flying in over the last few days' said Derek.

Chapter 19

The steak dinner Caroline served with mashed potatoes, peppers, onions, and runner beans in the evening in the small garden of No 79 was excellent. They ate alone as Concetta had gone to stay with a friend. Rob was grateful to be alone with Caroline for they could then talk freely. He enjoyed the Tempranillo wine but only drank a glass with the meal slowly.

'Did your parents name you Caroline after the Neil Diamond song; I remember that at discos years ago?'

'No' laughed Caroline 'I'm not that young the Beatles were not even famous when I arrived.'

'What am I thinking idiot, though still a good song.'

'Rob you seem distracted what's the matter?'

'They are going over to watch the villa tonight, Josette told me to stay with you, I don't like relying on those two.'

'You have to trust people Rob. Surely you do Josette. What is Randall like?'

Trust Josette he thought *yes but she is still recovering is it too much for her?* 'Strange on first impressions I thought he was some sort of crazy professor. Maybe he is but he has an encyclopaedic memory on the Russian Secret Service. But he's no field agent. I wonder what they are doing.'

'You will find out in the morning. Until we get to the villa there is nothing we can do. Now relax, that is what Josette wants you to do. Finish this wine' and she filled his glass.

'I was uptight like this before we landed in San Carlos Bay, it was the hours of waiting but once we were ashore it was OK.'

'What did you do then?'

'Well there were a lot of us all in the same boat, forgive the pun. We did have a few drinks the night before.'

'There you are now drink up.'

'Cheers' said Rob 'and drained half the glass.'

At twilight Josette and Derek set off for the For Sale or Rent ruin. By the time they arrived in the lane and parked it was dark. The half mile walk to the ruin Josette found tiresome with Derek, she thought *a herd of elephants would make less noise.* He shuffled along dragging his feet, within a hundred yards moaning about the distance.

Josette stopped as they passed through the gap in the old wall that had once been the boundary of the villa's garden now overgrown. She grabbed Derek by the arm. 'For Christ sake Derek' she hissed 'we are almost there keep fucking quiet. Even then he still managed to stumble on the steps.

At the viewing position Josette scanned the Russians Villa's pool area with her binoculars, it was well lit up. There were several people sat at the tables. A wooden dance platform had been laid for the Flamenco show and for any other similar things they had planned. The only person she recognised was the older blonde girl. There were more cars parked in the lane *must record the numbers* she thought.

'Ah!' said Derek puffing and panting 'all those stairs made it at last. Good view. Let's see now what have we here?' he said raising his binoculars. 'Hmm yes alright' he

150

murmured.

'Recognise anyone Derek?'

'Captain Mikhail Leonov, smoking the cigar.'

'Got him' said Josette. He had his long legs stretched out in front of him, and had an unfashionable pencil thin moustache.

'KGB, but small fry, probably someones aid or bag carrier. Now nine o'clock from his table, the one in the yellow shirt. Major Sergi Yuzhin '"Wolf" counter intelligence expert on the CIA, which could indicate something to do with the Americans. Anyone you have seen before?'

'Yes the blonde woman good looking, she was seen by Styles the first time he saw Judd after fifty years a few weeks ago.'

'What is she about thirty?' said Derek. 'Is there any resemblance to Judd? As Boris Antipov he was married had two children one was a daughter, could be her, sorry I don't know her name.'

'Shush' said Josette. Was it gravel she had heard crunching behind them. She listened intently holding her breath, all senses on alert. She drew her snub nosed .38 revolver, screwing on the long silencer slowly, careful not to make a sound or drop it. Cocking the hammer the well oiled mechanism was soundless.

She turned in one movement dropping in slow motion onto one knee. Facing the rear entrance their way in or out and where she sensed the sound had come from. Her senses filtered out the cicadas and the plant movement caused by a light southern breeze. She waited, nothing, finally releasing her grip on the pistol pointing it at the sky she gently released the hammer and stood up.

'All clear?' whispered Derek.

'I think so' said Josette. 'Any more new faces?'

'Yes indeed, one extremely revealing Tamara Minsker, see her, rather severe looking sat with Leonov now, about fifty I should think personal assistant to KGB General Viktor Semyonov, he seldom goes anywhere without her. Real old school started with the Cheka in the 1930's, joined SMERSH at its conception in 1943.'

'I thought that was fiction' said Josette.

'No it existed, counter espionage organisation *Smernesh* "Death to Spies". Stalin had it created to root out spies within the Soviet Armed Forces it was stood down after the war. Last time I heard old Semyonov was head of KGB training, must be in his seventies now.'

'Same age group as Judd.'

'Don't think we will learn much more' said Derek. 'Maybe we can find a bar on the way back.' Then he emitted a huge fart.

'Derek' said Josette 'control yourself I should think that could have raised the dead. And please keep the noise down going back to the car. Sound travels further at night.'

The second bottle of Tempranillo began to ease Rob's apprehension. He helped Caroline with the dishes. Then she went for a shower. He went back to the garden and the wine.

'Is there any of that left?' said Caroline coming from the shower in a cotton dressing gown a towel wound around her head.

Rob poured the remains of the bottle into her glass it was

near full. 'That's another dead one' he said gazing at the bottle.

'There is some San Miguel in the fridge if you would like one?'

'No thanks you should not mix your drinks' he said 'are you trying to get me drunk?'

'No' she said taking a drink of wine. 'Just trying to help you that's all I'm doing.'

The party that had been going on at another bungalow had died down to just some muted voices. It was near midnight Rob could not help his mind wandering back to how things were going at For Sale or Rent, would they be back yet? Whatever, he would just have to wait until the morning to find out if they had learnt anymore.

'I'm going to bed' said Caroline, getting up with her glass. 'Feel a bit bushed, don't be long Rob.'

'Draining his own glass, Rob sat staring into space wondering what tomorrow would bring. Going into the bungalow Rob switched off the lounge light where the sofa bed was, he could see light showing under the bedroom door, perhaps Caroline was reading he thought. He started to undress removing his shirt.

'Rob' called Caroline.

He moved over to the bedroom door opening it. Caroline lay naked on the bed her hair spread like a curtain across the pillows behind her head. 'In here please' she said patting the bed.

'I thought you were tired?'

'Yes I will be soon' she said smiling.

Rob removed the rest of his clothes and lay down beside her taking her in his arms. They both shivered as their bodies touched. Her breasts felt soft against his chest her hair smelt wonderful.

Chapter 20

1 October A.M.

The grey light of dawn began to reveal the outline of the bedroom as Rob woke. He felt refreshed it was the best night's sleep he had enjoyed for months even though it was not much over five hours. He knew why, it was down to the woman who lay beside him. He could hear her breathing gently. He reached out and stroked her soft hair.

'Hello darling' she murmured.

'Sorry I woke you.'

'Oh! I don't mind' she said reaching for him. 'I think at least part of you wanted me awake.'

An hour later Rob and Caroline were with Josette at the kitchen table in the higher bungalow, Derek was in the shower.

'It went well last night' explained Josette 'there are several more KGB men here. Derek identified most of them, and he suspects a general is at the villa. Although we did not see him his chief aid was there, and according to the expert he doesn't go anywhere without her.'

'This means we go tonight?' said Rob.

'Yes, have to as we still don't know the why.'

'Caroline is going to take her camera but she will only use it if it is easy.'

'Of course' said Josette 'don't take any risks.'

'Toward the middle end of the show' explained Rob 'I'm going to disappear and have a look round then find a cubby hole and hide. Once all is quiet I will get out. I will head for the For Sale or Rent place where you leave the car and you can pick me up from there.'

'You make sure you do' said Caroline.

'This must be Caroline' said Derek coming into the kitchen in a large pink fluffy dressing gown. 'What have we got to do?'

Josette glared at Derek. 'Don't you worry Caroline we will back him up.'

With nothing else to be said Rob and Caroline left them to their breakfast. After which they were going into Malaga to visit the Consul and check with London. By the time Josette expected to return, Rob and Caroline would have left for the rehearsal at the farm. Fernando was going to pick them up in the Cape from No 79.

It was near ten before Josette managed to get Derek into the Seat for the trip into Malaga after he had disposed of a huge breakfast. She was irritated by having to chivvy him along. *He's supposed to help* she thought *not be a bloody hindrance.*

The traffic along the coast road was heavy and it got steadily worse the closer they got to Malaga. 'Is it usual to be this hot?' said Derek wiping his red face with a huge handkerchief and he continued to moan. The car's fan was not good enough, how much longer would it take, he needed a toilet.

Ye Gods thought Josette *he's worse than a child.* His constant grumbling was distracting Josette, and she had a headache. She had not noticed the blue Ford Cortina, which had been following at a distance from Nerja. She had failed to keep a proper log the night before overwhelmed by Derek's revelations she had taken little notice of the extra vehicles parked in the lane. She had not changed the Seat yet as Rob had asked her to. They parked in a side street, not far from the British Consul building and walked to it.

Ten minutes later a red Volkswagen Golf drew up on the opposite side of the road directly adjacent to the Seat. The driver, a short man in T-shirt and jeans wearing sunglasses got out locked the car and walked away in the opposite direction that Josette and Derek had taken. Within two hundred yards he got into the back of a parked blue Ford Cortina.

In the consul building the print-out in the secure communications room from MI6 on the latest intelligence of IRA activity in southern Spain was waiting for them. It did not make good reading. There were an estimated eleven hard core Provos in the area. They also had known contacts with ETA the Basque Separatists.

'Under Andropov the Soviets supplied their Irish Republican friends with arms' said Derek. 'They even sent them plastic explosives they got from a source within the British Army of the Rhine.'

'You're telling me the Provo's have been blowing up our soldiers and politicians with explosives from our own army?'

'That's about the strength of it.'

'Would any of the Russians we have identified have contact with the Provos?'

157

'Most certainly, General Semyonov worked with Andropov before his downfall and out here I should think the Wolf and the Burner would have links to them, gang drug money is known to partly fund the Provos. In the murky world of Soviet Intelligence the KGB and gangsters go hand-in-hand.'

'Shit' said Josette. 'Rob was worried about this. Do you think we should cancel tonight seems their Irish chums could well be sat around the tables?'

'Not sure' said Derek 'if the Provos or ETA have people at the meeting it might not be wise, but would they, we just don't know.'

Josette's headache was getting worse. She bit her bottom lip in concentration. The doctors had warned her about too many headaches. *Should I contact the Firm tell them what we have planned. No it would take hours to get an answer.* She glanced at her watch twelve-thirty. They had time to get back to Nerja before Rob would leave with the troop. 'Come on Derek we had better go back and talk to Rob pronto.'

'What about lunch?' complained Derek.

'Your stomach will just have to wait, move it.'

From the blue Ford Cortina three men watched Josette and Derek hurry down the road. She opened the Seat and climbed in, Derek shuffling along behind got into the passenger seat by which time the engine was running and she had the car in gear. Sean Rice the man in the back seat with the sun glasses passed to the Burner Okudzhava a small remote control with the aerial already up. He switched it on. The Seat had already begun to move he smiled and said 'Adios' and pressed the button.

The force of the explosion rocked the Cortina. The Volkswagen Golf had 500 grams of the Czechoslovakian explosive Semtex under the fuel tank it had probably arrived in Spain from Libya. It blasted the Golf and Seat to fragments. Josette died instantly being closer to the blast, Derek a few seconds later his last thought was that he would miss lunch.

Chapter 21

1 October P.M.

It was just before eight in the evening Fernando turned the Cape into the lane that led to the Russians villa crunching into low gear. The old Bedford was fully loaded and her suspension had seen better days bottoming out on some of the bigger ruts. But he treated her gently going along at a walking speed.

Caroline and Rob sat close together; he squeezed her hand as the villa came into sight trying to reassure her.

Inside they were shown into a changing room that had a curtain to divide it, by the tall Russian girl who spoke good English. Rob helped Juan with all his paraphernalia finding their way along a corridor through a lounge out onto the patio and pool area. At the back on the makeshift stage Juan set up his gear. There were a few people moving about. The tall girl was there, the one who might be Judd's daughter thought Rob, and seemed to be in charge.

'You will be third event tonight' she said having come over to Juan.

'Si is good' he replied.

She tutted. 'Do you speak better English?' she said to Rob.

Rob nodded.

'Nine thirty you go on after the magic show and Mary Donovan our singer, then is you, and she will come on again to finish you understand?'

'Yes of course' said Rob.

It was still only twilight; Rob knew no one would be at the ruin opposite, five hundred yards away on its small hill now clearly outlined against the horizon of the sea. The sign For Sale or Rent was easy to read from here thought Rob. He went back inside the villa as Juan fiddled with his speakers and the gear, to get changed. The ground plan of the villa was imprinted on his mind he had spent hours studying it from the estate agents plan Hernandez had supplied.

Instead of taking the door to his left which led back to the changing room from the lounge Rob took the door straight ahead which he knew led to reception rooms. The first door leading off this corridor he knew was the dining room; people were coming and going from it for dinner. Rob strode purposely on, turning a corner in the corridor. The next large room was the library he had an idea this might be used for lectures or talks. He gently opened the door and went inside. There was no one there. A large presentation board stood on a stand, and desks in two rows were arranged before it, some of which still had pads and papers on them. He went no further, this would have to wait, the others would soon be wondering where he was, but he had found what he was looking for. He retraced his route back to the changing room.

'Juan is setting up, there are two acts on before us' Rob told Fernando on his return.

'Good we can watch, hurry por favor' said Fernando clapping his hands.

They were soon all out on the patio at the back. The

magic show was in full swing. All the tables were full and several guests were standing. Rob guessed there were about seventy people there. The Russians were almost childlike in their appreciation of the magician, hooting and shouting and applauding wildly.

Judd was sat with the tall blonde girl, while Mirkin had the younger girl sat on his lap, her skirt was as short as ever. Rob noticed Okudzhava headed in their direction his head moving backward and forward. The Burner thought Rob *he looks more like a snake to me.*

'The other night you not favour our company?' he said sidling up to Tina. She looked wide-eyed to Fernando.

'We were busy' said Caroline coming to Tina's rescue. 'It is not good to stay up late drinking, Fernando should never have agreed to it.'

Okudzhava lit a cigarette which he held in a holder. 'No matter' he said waving it in the air 'put on a good show tonight.' He then started rubbing his groin and grinning. His arm was grabbed from behind Krivitsky pulling him away, saying something lost in the hubbub of noise but Okudzhava nodded to him.

Rob took four pictures through the button hole behind the crowded tables catching, he hoped, some of the occupants in profile.

Next the singer came on and was introduced by the magician as Mary Donovan from Ireland. She ran through a selection of mostly Country and Western standards in a sweet voice. The Russians seemed to lap up this sample of American culture. Toward the end of the first half of her repartee she sang Spanish Eyes. Rob whispered to Caroline, 'she's doing our song.' Caroline gave him a forced smile he could tell she was apprehensive, whereas he now felt relaxed. With Mary moving onto her last number of the half "Jolene" they moved into position at the rear of the stage.

Coming on to the stage they were met with wild applause and foot stomping. Juan waited for silence and then started with the classical guitar and Isobel began her intense opener. They went on through Caroline's solo, then the three girls number, and onto Isobel and Fernando. Rob managed to take ten pictures standing at the back with Juan. When the three girls took to another routine which was suitably noisy with the crowd clapping along Rob slipped away, before the troop moved onto Isobel's final number and the end of the show.

All was quiet inside the villa, the lecture room was in darkness, Rob switched on the pencil torch. The curtains were still open so he was mindful he would have to be careful using it. Any flashes from the window might be picked up. He went to the presentation board, flicking back the plastic sheets one by one. On the third one at the top in the centre as if a heading he found two letters had not been rubbed off completely, the word started with a T and ended with a B there seemed room for seven letters in total. Going through the other sheets revealed nothing.

The papers Rob had seen on some of the desks had been cleared away. He checked the waste paper bin. *Ah bingo* he thought there were several screwed up sheets in it. Sat at a desk he flattened them out. Some had Russian words that meant nothing to him, he folded them up, Derek might be able to read them. On one piece there were some English words 'strike at Hofdi House from the sea' he put all the papers in his pocket.

He switched off his torch and made his way to the door. He opened it a fraction checking the corridor was empty, instead of turning right he turned left toward the kitchens. It might be an alternative exit to use later on. He found a chef there dressed in whites packing away utensils into boxes, he was a big man.

'Hola' said Rob 'pardon I'm with the Flamenco troop must have taken a wrong turn?'

'No worries' he replied in an Australian accent 'just go back the way you came mate there's your exit.'

'You're not Spanish?'

'You're dead right but neither are you.'

'Packing up?'

'That's right this bunch is moving out in the morning.'

'Odd all these Russians being here?'

'You ask a lot of questions for a Pommy Flamenco dancer' he said turning around staring at Rob.

'Well thanks' said Rob 'see you around' and left.

Back in the corridor he walked back toward the patio area he soon heard Mary Donovan singing "Talking in your Sleep". By now he thought the troop was probably changing maybe in the Cape already. It gave Rob a pang of loneliness which he shrugged off. He needed to find somewhere to hide and wait. He tried a few doors before he found a store room that would do. Inside in the dark the luminous dial of his watch told him it was just after eleven. As they were vacating the place tomorrow they would surely get to bed soon. He waited until after midnight and then eased the door open. The corridor was in darkness the lights had been turned off. He waited listening for five minutes. All the bedrooms were on the second floor.

He set off moving slowly along the corridor toward the lounge keeping close to the wall. The door to the lounge was open it was empty, as quietly as he could he slid the sliding door open that led onto the patio. *Drop over the wall and I'm away* he thought. They were waiting for him at For Sale or Rent, they would spot him shortly. He had to divert around the pool. It was then all the spotlights came on momentarily blinding him. He heard running steps. Someone shouted 'stop.'

He had almost cleared the pool when he was tackled low down around the legs and his assailant and Rob flew into the pool going under the water. Rob was up first he plucked the camera off his shirt and threw it over the wall. Somebody else had jumped in the pool. One man was moving toward him cutting off his escape. Rob lashed out at him with his fist he felt cartilage break and there was blood in the water. He had reached the edge of the pool and was about to heave himself out, another four steps and he could jump over the wall and drop into the lane. But a heavy blow struck the back of his head and everything spun down into blackness.

Chapter 22

2 October A.M.

It was near midnight when Fernando dropped Caroline and Concetta at Capistrano Village. They had all been asking her where Duncan was. But she just shrugged, saying one of the Russians had asked him to stay on. He would find his own way back later.

She lay awake in the bed she shared with Concetta, who was snoring gently. She was annoyed she had not been more help to Rob, but she had been so frightened. She muffled a sob and thought *this is no good.* Then got out of bed so as not to wake Concetta, in the kitchen she had a drink of water. It was two a.m. they might already be back; she put on her dressing gown and went outside walking up through the sleeping village until she could see the higher bungalow there was no car outside. She walked back deflated and lay on the sofa bed in the lounge knowing she would not sleep.

At four a.m. Caroline went through the same routine, there was still no car outside, now she was getting frantic. *Rob where are you?* she cried inside.

At eight a.m. Concetta woke, she wondered where Caroline was. Her question was soon answered she was on the sofa bed asleep in her dressing gown. She did not wake her but went on into the bathroom for a shower. When she came out she found Caroline in the kitchen, her eyes had

166

dark rings around them.

'Caroline, a bad night?' asked Concetta.

'Si' said Caroline; she was nursing a cup of tea. She had gone out again while Concetta was showering there was still no car. What could have happened to all three of them? She did not know what to do.

'A bad dream?' said Concetta.

'What?' said Caroline, Concetta's question had interrupted her chain of thought. They were always going to the Consul in Malaga that was it, she would phone them, and she would get dressed.

'Breakfast Caroline?'

'No, no thank you I'm going to shower and dress then I have to go out.'

These Ingles so intense thought Concetta and started making coffee.

Once again Caroline made her way to the higher bungalow. This time there was a car parked outside, but it was not the Seat they had been using. Maybe they had had car problems, yes that was it and she began to run. She knocked and went straight in calling out, 'Rob are you there?'

'Sorry Miss' said Ian Hamilton coming out of the kitchen. They both recognised each other but were not entirely sure who they were.

'I'm Ian Hamilton from the British Consul; I believe I saw you when we were taking Linda Styles into Malaga?'

It clicked with Caroline, when she had misread the situation and made a fool of herself. 'Caroline Gomez friend of Duncan's, I have been teaching him Flamenco.' She wondered just how much Hamilton knew, and if he had

167

picked up on her calling out to Rob.

'Oh! I see really Flamenco; did you know Susan West and Derek Randall?'

'Yes of course Susan, but not Derek very well.'

'You had better come and sit down' said Ian a grave look on his face.

'Just tell me' she said raising her voice 'please tell me what has happened?'

'All right, yesterday after leaving the Consul around one p.m. they were driving away when a car bomb exploded.'

'Dear God' said Caroline.

'They died instantly, it looks like an ETA attack that somehow went wrong, and they were innocent victims. In the wrong place at the wrong time jolly bad luck really.'

Jolly bad luck, what did he think it was a cricket match. 'What about Duncan?'

'No idea I was hoping you might know?'

Caroline shook her head. She recalled Rob saying he could not fathom why people always seemed one step ahead of him. And he could not trust people, in particular government officials. They all seemed to have their own agendas.

'Look there is a lot to sort out I have picked up some of their documents that I need to get the bodies released. Can I leave the keys with you, to this place, and when Duncan turns up if you could get him to give me a ring?'

'Yes anything to help' said Caroline.

With Hamilton gone she sat at the table and broke down her body racked with sobs. *Poor Josette blown to pieces,* she recalled Rob telling her this was a dangerous game he was not kidding.

She had not really believed him. 'Pull yourself together' she said out loud and wiped her nose on some kitchen towel. *I will be no help to Rob like this.* She found an open bottle of Jerez Brandy and poured a good measure into a glass and gulped it down, it made her cough, but fortified her a little.

She started to think more clearly. As Josette and Derek died yesterday afternoon they were not there to cover Rob last night. So where was he? The last place she knew him to have been was the villa, so she would go there but how? On the kitchen work top beside the draining board she noticed the keys to the E-type and said 'yes.'

She hurried back down to No 79 and picked up her hand bag, Rob's holdall and some cash. Back at the higher bungalow she removed the cover from the E-type, rolled it up and put it in the back through the rear door along with Rob's holdall.

Behind the wheel she took a deep breath and concentrated remembering what Rob had said. 'Push the choke up to the top hold it there, switch on the ignition wait for the pump to stop ticking' which she did then pressed the starter button. The engine started instantly she allowed herself a thin smile of triumph. Gently she warmed the engine for a couple of minutes. Then cutting the choke back to half way and engaged first gear releasing the handbrake the car lurched down over the kerb heavily. 'Have to watch that Caroline, be gentle.'

At the local garage, she put fifty litres of petrol into the E-type, working it out in her head to be about ten gallons. The fuel gauge then read just under three quarters full.

Driving up to the villa it became obvious the Russians

had gone there were no cars parked. And when she tried the door it was locked. A notice on it read it was available to rent there was a contact number for a Malaga estate agent. Caroline walked along the side lane toward the ruin called For Sale or Rent. She hoped Rob might be somewhere nearby, but why would he stay here, unless he was injured. She kicked something with her shoe and looking down saw the miniature camera the same as the one Rob had given to her, she bent down and picked it up. It had to be Rob's she thought, which meant he had to have got out, or had he thrown it here from the patio.

'Perdon senorita' a man's voice interrupted her thoughts she had not heard his approach from the direction of For Sale or Rent. She clutched the camera tightly.

He was wearing a panama hat dressed in a short sleeve white shirt and jeans. He touched the brim of his hat in deference to her. He had an engaging smile illuminated by his very white teeth. 'What have you found?' he said in good English.

'Who are you?' she asked.

'Policia, to be precise CESID you know of us?' he said removing his hat.

'Yes' said Caroline 'secret police.'

He did a little bow. 'They do not call us that now so much. What are you looking for?'

Caroline did not answer.

'I could arrest you senorita. But I will not' he sighed. 'It is always better to have cooperation, do you not find so?'

Caroline still did not answer.

'No matter I will tell you a little story. Please to come into the shade' he said indicating some nearby trees.

Caroline moved into the shade warily keeping her distance from him.

'Let me introduce myself I am Captain Ferdinand Hernandez' he paused hoping she would tell him her name. 'Yesterday' he continued 'there was a bombing in Malaga. Two Britons died in it. The official press release says an ETA accident. This is not so those Britons were working for MI5, and forensics have established the bomb was detonated remotely, which means they were the target and murdered. I had met the woman before Susan West, but not the man, when I met her she was with Duncan Dixon.' He went on to explain the stake out and then waited.

Caroline looked at the ground, and then at him, finally making up her mind. 'Do you know where Rob is?'

'Rob who is Rob?'

'Duncan Forbes Dixon was a cover name. His real name is Rob, Robin Nicolson. I'm Caroline Gomez a friend of his. He got into this villa last night.' It was like a flood gate opening as she told him everything, and then handed him the camera.

'These Russians have now killed three people whatever their motives it must be important to them' reflected Hernandez. He smiled at her. 'Is that your car?' he pointed at the E-type 'what a beauty.' They walked back down the lane to it. He looked around it touching the bullet holes. 'There was a report of a red car such as this seen near where some heavily armed Irish men got killed on a mountain road in the Sierra Nevada?'

Caroline nodded, 'Yes Rob thought that somehow his movements were compromised. What has happened to him Captain, should we search the villa?'

'With the keys from the estate agent I have already been inside there is no sign of your friend. As to what happened to him I do not know Senorita, but I will find out. I think you should hide this car like Senor Nicolson did, perhaps not in the same place can you do that?'

'Yes Captain I think so.'

'Good and call me Hernandez' he handed her a card from his wallet. 'If you need me I can be reached on these numbers.'

Hernandez watched Caroline turn the E-type around noting it was heavy work for her, and then drive away.

Caroline drove the Jaguar to the farm which she and Rob had used for rehearsals, parking the car in a barn. The roof was in bad condition but the E-type was invisible there. From the farm she walked a mile back to the main road and caught the local bus into Nerja, getting off at Capistrano village. She walked up to the higher bungalow but it was locked as she had left it. She was in a little better spirits as she felt now she had an ally in Hernandez.

Chapter 23

3 October

Opening one eye Rob closed it in an instant. Something was far too bright. His head felt hollow and throbbed with dull pain. He wanted to go back to the embracing blackness. Yet something was nagging him. A name came into his mind he mouthed Caroline. He started singing about sweet Caroline in his mind but it hurt too much. Then he had a picture of a tall, slim dark haired woman beautiful in a red and black dress with lots of lace. She would be worried. But why was she worried?

He opened one eye again. The light was blinding but he kept it open and then opened the other one they began to focus. The room, or more accurately he was to learn, the cell, furniture consisted of a bucket in one corner and the bed he was lying on, the springs covered by a thin mattress and he was covered by two foul smelling blankets. He pushed the blankets away, put his legs over the side of the bed and sat up. His head swam, but he stayed upright resisting the temptation to lie down again. It helped putting his hands flat on the bed either side of him.

The light was coming from a single bare bulb hanging on a cord six inches from the ceiling which now hardly seemed that bright. The room was ten foot long by six wide. High up near the ceiling on the end wall was a window two feet square which was casting grey light into the room. At the other end wall was the door. *Well I don't rate the accommodation* he thought. Looking down he saw he was still dressed in his black Flamenco shirt and trousers. His feet were bare and dirty. There was nothing in his pockets and his watch was gone.

The spinning of his head had all but stopped. It was coming back to him what had happened, he had almost got away. How had they found out he was there? *Now where am I?* He touched the back of his head his hair was matted with dried blood. He pressed it gently; it was sore but did not bleed. He stood on the bare concrete floor which felt cold. The walls were painted a dirty grey. The door on closer examination was wooden with what looked like a spy hole in it. Two steps and he was beside it he tried the handle it was locked. He walked to the other end three and a half strides. High up in one corner was a small barred window. He stood on the bed but was still unable to look through the window he could barely even reach it with his hands. There was no chance to look through it. *Is this it?* he thought. 'Hello' he shouted 'I'm awake you morons.'

He walked back to the door and put his ear to it listening. He could hear nothing. He looked in the bucket it was empty. He urinated in it. His underwear was dry. How long had he been unconscious he wondered. He looked at his arms for tell tale signs. The left had a bruise on the inside of the forearm; it looked like a needle mark.

Nothing to do but wait, don't get worked up chum. Clear your mind do something mundane. In his head he started doing weapon drills.

SLR rifle. Self Loading Rifle designed by Fabrique Nationale d' Herstal of Belgium known as the FN manufactured under licence in Britain came into service with UK forces 1954. Fires a 7.62 round twenty round magazine muzzle velocity 2,700 feet per second.

Stoppages, weapon stops firing cock, hook working parts to the rear no rounds in the magazine none in the chamber empty magazine change magazine release working parts carry on firing. Weapon stops again after one or two rounds, cock, hook working parts to the rear rounds in the magazine and in the chamber. Gas turn the gas setting down by two clicks carry on firing.

By the time Rob had finished with the SLR and the GPMG, the General Purpose Machine Gun, and started on the SMG, the Sub Machine Gun, the turning of a key in the door lock stopped his flow.

The door opened inwards. Two guards stood framed in the doorway dressed in light green uniforms the shoulder boards of the jackets had GB on them, Rob knew that was KGB. On their peaked caps was a single red star. At their hips both carried pistols in holsters. Rob stood, one immediately gestured to him to sit. The other moved momentarily out of sight then came back with a tray; he placed it on the floor and with his boot slid it into the cell.

'Ah! Room service' said Rob.

There was no response from them. The door closed with a bang, and the lock turned.

Rob picked up the tray and put it on the bed. A steel mug held some liquid that smelt like coffee and was lukewarm. There was a bowl of what looked like dirty water with dubious bits floating in it. Beside it was a hunk of grey bread. There was a plastic spoon. He took a drink from the mug there was a faint taste of coffee.

He nibbled a corner of the bread it was dry and hard. He dipped a corner into the bowl the contents of which smelt like rotten cabbage, but it did soften the bread which made it more palatable.

'Well that was breakfast roll on lunch' he said. It was good to hear the sound of his voice. He examined the mug, bowl, tray and spoon. There were no marks on any of them. The tray was fairly heavy might turn as a weapon but with two of them he doubted he would have any chance.

He started thinking of Caroline, wondering what she was doing. Another good woman he would lose. But he quickly realised it would do him no good thinking about that. *Concentrate on the here and now. How long have I been here?* He looked up at the high window it seemed as if it was lighter now so it was later in the day. He considered standing the bed on one end, he would have to lean it against the wall, and climb up it to the window then he might be able to see outside.

The key turned in the lock again the two guards were back one held a pistol, the other had handcuffs he gestured to Rob to put his hands together out in front of him. He did so and the handcuffs were snapped on him. 'Good time for exercise' he said.

Outside the three of them walked along a bare corridor the flagstones were cold on Rob's feet, they rang with the sound of the guards boots. Single bulbs in a row along the ceiling lit the corridor. To both sides there were more doors like the one in his cell. At the end of the corridor a flight of stairs led up to another corridor at the top they turned left, at the end was a door one guard opened it while the other led Rob in.

'Oh no comrades, remove the handcuffs' said Martin Judd, he was sat behind a large wooden table. He wore the same shade of green uniform as the guards but with a silver star on the boards and blue stars on the collar of the jacket, the uniform of a colonel. The guards did as he asked. 'Wait outside please I will have no trouble.'

'Please sit Duncan Forbes Dixon or is it Robin Nicolson, late of Her Majesty's Royal Marines?' said Judd indicating the chair to his front.

Rob did not sit but walked over to the large picture window. The view was of mountains marching away in the distance clothed with pines and framed by higher snow capped peaks.

'A fine view my friend, welcome to the Soviet Union they are the Urals we are a thousand miles east of Moscow.

Rob sat down and stared at Judd.

'Good that is better. You see' he waved toward the window 'there is no escape. There is no real need of handcuffs. Now if you are sensible and cooperate life will be tolerable, who knows one day you might even be exchanged, it happens sometimes. If on the other hand you are intransigent life will be grim. All you have to do is answer my questions. Why were you and your friends so interested in our meeting?'

Rob considered talking. But instead almost on reflex said; 'Robin Nicolson, Marine' followed by his service number.

'Ah! Bravo, name, rank, and number. Invoking the Geneva Convention, yet sadly for you we are not at war and you no longer wear the uniform of Her Majesty's Royal Marines. So it cuts no ice here. You would be better to answer my questions and life will improve.'

Rob repeated name, rank, and number.

'To tell the truth I half expected this' said Judd 'stiff upper lip and all that. By the way I omitted to tell you we liquidated your comrades, Miss West and Derek Randall so no one even knows you are missing. Nothing further to say?'

Rob repeated name, rank, and number.

'Comrades' called Judd the guards came in. 'Return our friend here to his cell, make life a touch more unpleasant for him.'

Chapter 24

The guards put the handcuffs back on Rob and dragged him back to the cell. There they removed the blankets and left him in the handcuffs.

'Bastards' he shouted as the door slammed shut and the key turned in the lock. The sun was starting to sink Rob guessed as the light from the small window had dimmed. The cell had been cold before now it felt freezing. He curled up on the mattress trying to keep warm. But he was soon shaking with cold. He tried some physical jerks as best he could. He knew he was in real danger of exposure although he doubted they would let him die. As part of him tried to combat the cold, another part analysed his situation. Was he better off playing Judd's game? *Maybe I made a mistake stonewalling. I need to be clever and play his game. Survive and get home.* He said those last four words over and over.

It was a long cold night. Rob got precious little sleep, he had to stay awake to stay alive he could not trust those dozy guards. But at last light started coming through the small window, and the temperature rose only a few degrees but it was enough he judged to let him sleep.

It was as if he had only shut his eyes when the door was flung open and he was dragged to his feet by his jailers. Then out along the corridor unable to keep up with their fast pace his feet took a battering on the flag stones.

'Oh! Comrades I said a little unpleasant, you see Nicolson they are overzealous like children' said Judd sniggering. 'Remove the handcuffs.'

Robs arms and shoulder joints throbbed with pain as blood was able to circulate as normal. There was a fire in the grate, Rob moved toward it to warm his hands, leaving bloody footprints on the flag stones.

'Now then Nicolson we start again. Why were you and your comrades so interested in our meeting?'

Rob concentrated he blinked away his tiredness he took some time to think before he spoke. 'We would not have been it was only your murder of Commander Styles, your old ship mate that drew our attention. We questioned your motives Martin Judd' Rob spoke slowly.

'That was unfortunate, poor Mat, so you know my background?'

'Yes did you know you got a posthumous mention in dispatches for your actions during the air raid on Barcelona? How did you get away?'

'It was easy, I was going to defect it was planned. The air raid was just a bonus that I took advantage of and it covered my trail.'

Rob was pleased Judd was vain, that much was clear. *I might be on to something* he thought. 'Commander Styles thought you had "red" tendencies as he put it, when you shared a cabin on the Hood. As we know he was right.'

'Not to start with when I first joined the Royal Navy. I was keen to be a model naval officer, to serve the King and Empire. But the way people were treated by the establishment infuriated me. I was shaken to the core by the Invergordon Mutiny in thirty-one. I was only a snot nose subbey on the cruiser Norfolk, there the men who were more articulate, they called them ringleaders even though they were promised amnesty, they were thrown out of the service reduced to beggary. Just for complaining. Some of the lower deck had their wages reduced by a quarter. I never trusted the navy or the government after that. The men were wonderful it was no surprise some of them joined the Communist Party. Do you know that idiot of a king back then thought it was a Bolshevik plot. Not that they were being crucified by the banks and western capitalism. I met one or two of these men in Spain fighting with the International Brigade; I became convinced they were right, and that only the Soviet Union was really supporting them.' He stopped and smiled thinly. 'You are clever Nicolson, I can see I must not underestimate you, it is not me who is being interrogated.'

'You asked me why we were interested, I told you.'

'So you went to Spain just because Styles reported seeing me?'

'No, not really, I was sent out for R and R after a nasty mission. The Styles case was a low priority most felt it was likely to be a waste of time he was a bit touched.'

'Touched, explain?'

'They felt he had gone doolally, he was asking us to believe he had seen someone who died fifty years ago now with a bunch of Russians.'

'You arrived in Spain what then?'

'Styles presented a conundrum.'

'In what way?'

'Styles was a keen photographer, he followed you to the other villa took some good photographs of you, Krivitsky,

Mirkin, Okudzhava and the rest. And he sent them by post to the UK before you killed him.'

'Ah! We were not quick enough.'

You cold bastard thought Rob *no remorse for your old ship mate.* 'The Firm soon identified you and the others and we were told to watch you and try and find out what you were up to. All you old guard fellows, even then they gave it a low priority.'

Judd nodded. 'Comrade' he shouted one of the guards entered. 'Some breakfast for our friend here. Nicolson you watched us how?'

'From the ruin with the sign on it, For Sale or Rent.'

'You came in with the Flamenco people did they know of your mission?'

'No, a contact told us they were going to perform for you. I volunteered to join them, having done a bit on the stage before. They, the Flamenco groups, have a problem these days getting enough Spanish men to join, that part was easy.'

'And what did you learn?'

'A few more faces, got some papers from the waste paper bin, you really should be more careful, but you know this.'

Breakfast arrived. There was real hot coffee with sugar and milk and fresh croissants and butter.

'Tuck in' said Judd 'I have had mine. What other forces know of this?'

'The other agents filed a report to the firm so they know. What they make of a lot of Russian has-beens meeting in Spain who knows, but they have more up to date intelligence to go on.'

'What do you mean has-beens?'

Maybe a sore spot there thought Rob. 'As far as Derek was concerned, all of you, even General Semyonov, no longer have much influence with the Gorbachev regime.'

Judd got up folded his arms across his chest and walked to the window. He lowered his head thinking.

'Who was Tonya Antipov?' said Rob 'Did you take her name?'

'Asking questions again Nicolson?'

Rob shrugged. 'I don't imagine it is all that important now.'

'Tonya was instrumental in getting me away when I deserted. She was devoted to the cause in Spain.'

'She got caught?'

'Yes she did. I think that is enough for today. Comrades' he called.

'Do you think I could have my blankets back, maybe a pullover, and my shoes my feet are really suffering?'

'My, my, a veritable shopping list.' The guards came in. Judd spoke to them in Russian pointing at Rob's feet. They took Rob back to the cell this time without handcuffs.

Chapter 25

Two days after Hernandez had seen Caroline at the Villa he sat in an interview room in the CESID headquarters in Malaga. Before him across the desk sat Ruban Okudzhava he looked like he had been in the ring with Mike Tyson. His nose was strapped up with surgical tape, his left eye was badly swollen almost shut and around it the skin was black, red and yellow. Beside him sat a Spanish lawyer, beside Hernandez sat a female translator of Russian. She was young, a girl no more than a student really. *Not ideal for this* thought Hernandez.

Hernandez had collected a lot of data on the Russian's movements from airline passenger lists that had left Spain in the last forty-eight hours. They had been filtered down to Russian names, passport details and flights to Russia. This resulted in the identification of Boris Krivitsky and Anna Chekhova who had flown to Berlin from Barcelona, Anna was twenty-two he guessed the one with the short skirts Marcus had enthused about. Viktor Semyonov and Tamara Minsker had flown from Madrid to Moscow; Grace Antipov had been on the same Saturday morning flight. Major Sergi Yuzhin had flown to Paris from Malaga late on the Friday night. Mikhail Leonov had flown to Reykjavik from Barcelona early on Saturday morning. There was no record of Vladimir Mirkin, Ruban Okudzhava, or Martin Judd having left. Okudzhava had been identified as resident in Marbella.

He also had a report of a blue Ford Cortina being in the vicinity of the bombing in Malaga with three men in it, one was thought to be Okudzhava. The pictures developed from the miniature camera Caroline Gomez had found had not been all that helpful, apart that is from one that was good and clear that identified from Interpol files Sean Rice a known IRA assassin at the Russian meeting sat with Okudzhava. The bomb attack in Malaga had the hallmarks of the Provo's. Hernandez did not like foreigners conducting their battles on the streets of Spain. Thus he had given orders for the arrest of Okudzhava and Rice.

The day after Caroline Gomez had telephoned him it was obvious the Senorita was distressed over the whereabouts of Robin Nicolson. There was little he could do to help her; he told her checks had shown he had not flown out of Spain. But he could have been taken over the border into France or Portugal. He had put out alerts for the three Mercedes cars being used by the Russians. He did not tell her he had considered contacting MI5 but decided against it, they could contact him. It was their agents who were in trouble. Other than that he had said he was sure Nicolson was alive.

'Ruban Okudzhava what do you know about the car bombing in Malaga?' Hernandez began the interview speaking in English.

The lawyer stiffened in his seat.

'Nothing' said Okudzhava.

Hernandez placed a photograph on the table of Okudzhava and Rice clearly talking during the entertainment at the villa near Nerja. 'This man you are talking with' said Hernandez placing his finger on him 'is Sean Rice he has been identified in a Ford Cortina near the scène of the bomb attack. He is a known member of the IRA. What are you talking to him about in this picture, taken only hours after the attack?'

'I was at a party he was at.'

'My client is not responsible for who was invited to the party Captain.'

Hernandez had wondered about the lawyer, why a Spaniard? Surely a representative from the Russian Consul would carry more weight. He smiled at the lawyer. 'You are not answering my question Okudzhava, what are you talking with Rice about?'

'The show.'

'And the show was?'

'An Irish girl singing, maybe she was a friend of his.'

'How did you know she was Irish?'

'Her name was Mary Donovan.'

Hernandez withdrew the photograph and replaced it with a picture of Robin Nicolson. 'Do you know this man?'

'No' said Okudzhava.

'Please take a better look.'

'I have never seen him before.'

'That is not true' said Hernandez 'do not lie to me. You saw him when you met the Flamenco troop in Fuengirola at' he glanced down at his notes 'the hotel Las Palmeras you went out drinking with the girls from the troop.'

'No he was....' began Okudzhava.

'No he was what?' said Hernandez.

Okudzhava remained silent.

His single eye like some strange Cyclops bothered

Hernandez emitting hate. 'I think you should talk with your lawyer he should advise you of the powers CESID has in matters of state security, you could rot in prison for years without trial bear that in mind.'

Hernandez got up with the interpreter and left the interview room. He let her go joking 'our friend speaks good English after all but thank you for coming.'

Ten minutes later he returned to the interview room. The case was beginning to irritate him, taking too much of his time. He had already postponed one golf match. 'Right' he said 'you either talk Okudzhava or go to prison, I am a busy man.'

Okudzhava remained silent.

'My client has nothing further to say Captain' said the lawyer with pleading eyes.

No doubt you have better things to do thought Hernandez, feeling a pang of sympathy for the lawyer. 'As you wish, I will have to alert the Russian authorities that we are holding you as a murder suspect.'

'I don't want that' said Okudzhava.

'Found your voice, no matter what you want, it is required by law as you are a foreign national.'

Chapter 26

Back in his cell Rob found that he had everything he had asked for. The blankets were back but smelt no better. There was a fur lined three quarter length body warmer, and his Flamenco boots. He was happiest about the boots the steel toes were an effective weapon. Yet as he sat on the bed he felt he had missed something important. He could not fathom what. His brain had taken too long to de-frost.

He thought about escape. Surprise was the key, but even with that element it would be impossible to achieve with two guards. He would have to take his chance when it came. He did some exercises press-ups, star jumps, squat-thrusts, but sit-ups were out with the rough concrete floor.

Next he put the bed up on its end leant it against the wall and climbed up the delicate structure to the window. He got a brief glimpse of the outside; he did not hang there long before the bed slid away and clattered to the floor. He saw what looked like a small square closed in on three sides by buildings one of which he was in, there were vehicles parked in the middle. There was something else, the three sides looked like cloisters, arches supported by columns it was surely some kind of monastery. But then in Russia they used a lot of old religious buildings for other purposes. The churches had been restricted for years under the Soviets.

Rob was fed again as the light was beginning to go. A bowl of a meat stew, with coffee, cream and sugar, brought in by the two guards. He passed another cold night but tolerable with the blankets and body warmer.

Lying there in the early morning, his breath easy to see in the frosty air as he exhaled, Rob thought over the interview with Judd. He was not so clever this KGB Colonel; he had not picked up on how they had found the second villa when we could not find the first. And that CESID had helped them.

'I hope you had a better night' said Judd, as Rob walked into his office the next morning escorted by the two guards.

'Better but not the Ritz' said Rob.

'Yes of course' said Judd not commenting on Rob's attempt at a joke. Instead he looked down at a pad in front of him.

Rob thought he had not taken notes on the first two sessions, why now? Although likely there was a hidden mike.

Judd flicked through the pages. 'When you left the Flamenco show at the villa what did you do?'

'As I told you I explored some rooms found the library come lecture room, found nothing.'

'Other than the papers in the waste paper bin' said Judd.

'That's right, I poked around a bit, the chef told me you were leaving soon. I then' Rob laughed 'hid in a store room. Waited until I thought everyone had gone to bed, and was on my way out, well you know the rest.'

Judd took a newspaper from the desk drawer. 'This is the Spanish edition of the Daily Mail about a week old' he slid it across to Rob.

The headlines read. *Two Brit's killed in ETA bomb outrage in Malaga. Susan West and Derek Hammond on holiday died instantly as they pulled away in their car next to a massive car bomb.....* 'Why are you showing me this?' said Rob.

'You did not mention that Hammond was MI6?'

Rob shrugged. 'What does it matter?'

'I will be the judge of what matters' said Judd 'MI6 espionage and MI5 counter espionage two different remits?'

'I was told we owed SIS a favour, as I was going out to Spain on R and R Styles was low priority, I could look into it, a minor matter.'

One of the guards came in with a tray.

'Your breakfast Nicolson smells good.'

Rob was impressed there was a fried egg, OK it had gone hard and some sausages, still the awful grey bread. Rob started eating.

'Why should CESID arrest one of our men in Spain?' said Judd.

Lucky Rob had a full mouth, he had time to think. 'Excuse me; yes CESID isn't that Spanish Military Intelligence?'

'Yes' said Judd 'they also have a counter intelligence branch.'

'Maybe they know the bomb attack was not ETA, don't they have an anti-terrorist section as well. You didn't use semtex did you, you did?' Rob laughed. 'That might have given the game away.'

'That could be' mused Judd. 'You would not have been working with them?'

'Wish we had' said Rob 'London would not have agreed to that, trusting the "Don's," not on old sport.'

'Perhaps you and Miss West did it on your own initiative?'

'Do you know how long I have been with the Firm officially? No, I'll tell you less than twelve months and I wish I had never joined. Susan was on R and R as well, she was recovering from a stroke. No we wanted an easy life, but there was a mystery about Styles we had to solve'

Judd sat back in his chair thinking. *Was Nicolson trying to be clever, was he a Decoy deliberately entering their organisation inviting capture? The risk level was rising. Time was running out.* He wrote one word in Russian at the bottom of his notes *vypoineniye* execution.

'Comrades' he called, the two guards came in. He spoke in Russian to them one went away. 'Finish your breakfast Nicolson the guard will take you back to your cell, you have been most helpful, I have a pressing engagement.'

Chapter 27

6 October A.M.

Whatever had taken Judd away he had been in a hurry, he had left his pad on the table open. Rob was eating his breakfast he tried to read it upside down. It was in Russian it might just as well have been in double Dutch thought Rob it meant nothing to him. He wondered why Judd had rushed away *was it something I said? These sausages are good* he thought. *Hang on you fool they are acorn ones, do they have them in Russia?* And yes the thing that had been nagging at him yesterday he could not put his finger on but could now. *Do you get croissants in Russia, maybe in Moscow but not in a KGB prison in the Urals? It's time to give it a go* thought Rob. There was only one guard, the smaller one of the two. He was looking out of the window not even watching Rob. Should he make a grab for his pistol from behind? On the other hand his coffee mug was near full, it wasn't boiling hot but hot enough.

He stood up mug in hand 'Comrade.'

The guard turned around and got the mug of coffee in his face. Rob followed up with a lashing kick his steel tipped boot catching the guard's knee cap. He doubled over clutching his knee omitting a cry Rob's next kick caught him in the groin and was the best of the blows. He heard the air whistle out of him. Rob punched him on the side of the head with his fist and he was down. He pulled the pistol out of his holster a 9mm Makarov rolled him over and stripped off his jacket, and put it on. He was out cold, but Rob still handcuffed his hands behind his back. He picked up Judd's pad from the table and stuffed it in his jacket pocket.

Moving to the door Rob listened, nothing. He opened it a fraction the corridor was empty. He moved quickly along it passing the steps that led down to the lower level and the cells. At the end was another door, he eased it open, it led out into the cloisters. He turned right and ran to the end where there was another right corner that led to a dead end of a small wall. Looking out onto the square where the vehicles were parked there was no sign of life. Rob jumped over the wall the drop only about eight foot, but he landed on uneven ground and felt his ankle go over.

'Shit' he cried 'that's all I need.' He knew he had damaged it. He tried his weight on it the pain was sharp. He hobbled toward the nearest car a Mercedes sports, tried the door handle it was locked. He tried the saloon beside it the door opened. The keys were in the ignition. He got in and turned the key the engine spun but did not fire. He glanced at the gauges; fuel half a tank, a light was blinking. Heater plugs must be a diesel, wait until the light goes out.

There was a shout. He glanced up a man was pointing toward him from the cloisters directly to the front. 'Come on' he said. The light blinked off Rob turned the key again the engine burst into life with the familiar diesel rattle. He moved the automatic shift into reverse and spun the car around, stopping, into drive and he was away, wheels and tyres sliding fighting for grip.

The old monastery lay deep in a narrow valley with mountains rising high around it. The road led up and away through trees to a ridge line where it disappeared. He drove fast the rear wheel's skidding for grip on the loose surface of what was not much more than a track. Crack, crack shots rang out. There was an explosion of glass behind him as the rear screen shattered. But he was in the trees now shielded from the monastery. Rob eased off a bit he did not want to lose control. Reaching the ridge line the track emerged onto a T junction with a tarmac road. Which way he mused, glancing left and right nothing, he turned left and accelerated away.

In a mile or so he shot across a narrow bridge the road kept descending Rob wondered where he was, in Spain for certain the Pyrenees or Sierra Nevada? He was glad to see no vehicles following when he took brief glances. The car clock told him it was nine forty a.m. He came into a hamlet a small cluster of houses, a ski lift leading up toward a towering mountain. Then he was through it, no sign posts.

Ten minutes later he came to another T junction there were signs now it was the N324 to the left Granada to the right Almeria. He turned left accelerating hard. The sign had said forty-five kilometres to Granada. It was a good dual carriageway road. He eased back to about seventy mph. The high peaks of the Sierra Nevada were receding behind him. He allowed himself a smile. *The Urals Russia what an idiot, you almost fell for that one pal. What am I going to do when I get to Granada?* he thought. Drive onto Nerja, no that was out with the rear screen missing that was asking to be stopped. He needed somewhere to hole up to think and now his mobility was compromised with the ankle.

Coming into Granada, he noticed a sign post for the

Alhambra parking, he could see a large car park in the distance, and he took the slip road to it. There were a lot of cars and coaches in the park ideal to ditch the Mercedes. He parked, switched off. He took off the jacket and removed the wallet from it, inside were about 10,000 pesetas about fifty pounds, nothing else he wanted so he dropped the wallet on the floor and pocketed the notes. He took the gun off the passenger seat where he had placed it. He checked the Makarov over, the magazine was full eight rounds. He thought about leaving it in the car, but it fitted fairly well into one of the jacket pockets so he kept it. He ripped the shoulder boards off the jacket. He searched the inside of the car, in the glove box he found a useful road map and a pair of sunglasses which he took.

Out of the car Rob hobbled over to the Alhambra entrance. There were some local buses there that ran down to the city. *Need change for that* he thought. There was a refreshment stall where he could change a note he joined the queue. Just as he did he noticed a black Mercedes 500 SE the same model as he had been driving come into the car park going fast followed by a Citroen. There were six men in the two cars Rob was sure one of them was the bigger guard. They soon spotted the Mercedes Rob had abandoned and were quickly checking inside. Rob still had the keys in his pocket he dropped them in a rubbish bin. *How the hell had they got here,* thought Rob. *The bloody motor must have had a tracker.* The local buses did not seem in a hurry to move one driver was reading a paper and two others were out of their cabs talking. Rob needed cover. Nearby was a tour group Americans by the sound of them, Rob moved over to it.

'Right you guys' said the plump lady leader 'I have the tickets for you all timed so you can enter now down there' she pointed toward some turnstiles. 'You have three hours in this world heritage site so enjoy, now come and get your tickets, wow not all at once.'

Rob thrust his hand into the melee and was rewarded with a ticket. He moved off to the entrance with a group of the Americans.

'Don't remember you on the bus?' said one peroxide blonde middle aged woman.

'Late joiner honey' said Rob in an awful American southern accent.

Inside the palace conclave he lost the group and found a seat, close to the Palacio del Partal, a pavilion with an arched portico, the building reflected in the still water on an adjacent pool. But Rob's mind was not on the Moorish wonders of Spain.

Why are they chasing me, why did they go to such lengths to try and convince me I was in Russia? None of it made sense. *Why kill Josette and Derek?* It all felt like overreaction. *They must think I know more than I do.* Rob knew he needed help. But who could he trust? He ruled out the British Consul and the Firm, he needed help now, they would take too long to react and he did not entirely trust them. There was only one person he was willing to trust and that was Caroline. He did not like the idea there was still too much risk but there was no alternative with less risk, and he wanted her close for her own sake.

He made his way slowly to the exit hobbling along. At the gift shop he bought a gaudy shirt with the Alhambra printed on it and a baseball cap emblazoned with Granada. In the toilets he got rid of the jacket and changed into the Alhambra shirt wrapping the gun in his black Flamenco shirt which he put in the carrier bag they had given him in the shop. Putting on the sun glasses as well he looked every inch the tourist.

Exiting through the shop, he got onto a bus for the city. As the bus drove out of the car park he noticed both Mercedes were gone *must have had a spare set of keys* he thought. The Citroen was still there, two men were sat in it watching people. They gave no sign of having spotted Rob. It was only a mile or so to the Cathedral Square where Rob got off. He moved as fast as he could into the maze of narrow streets surrounding the Cathedral he didn't spot any of the Russians but there were hundreds of people milling around. He found a small coffee shop and sat down ordering cappuccino and cake. 'Perdone telefono por favour?' he asked the waiter when it arrived.

'Si' he said pointing inside to the bar.

Rob ate his cake and drank the coffee, then went inside. He dialled the area code for Nerja then the number of the bungalow. He knew it was a long shot. The phone was slow connecting, with lots of background buzzing, but then it started to ring. He let it ring and ring but no answer. Next he dialled 003 for the directory service and got the number of the Nerja Club Hotel. It was the only way he could think of getting a message to her. Reception answered. He explained he was trying to contact Caroline Gomez, at first the receptionist did not sound enthusiastic, until he said it was an urgent family matter. He gave his real name and the cafe's number.

There was nothing to do now but wait. He stayed in the

bar and consumed three more coffees, a toasted sandwich, and had started on a beer before he heard the telephone ring. One of the waiters picked it up. Looked around the bar and gestured to Rob 'Telefono Senor?'

'Hola' said Rob full of nervous anticipation, would it be Caroline?

'Rob is that you?' said Caroline.

The relief was intense all he could say was 'Thank you.'

'Are you all right Rob?'

'I need your help can you get to Granada today?'

'Yes, yes it will take a while but yes.'

He told her he would wait for her in the Plaza Bib-Rambla near the Cathedral. If she had any trouble she could phone the cafe and leave a message. He would check with them every hour.

Chapter 28

Caroline held the receiver in mid-air smiling; she was in the higher bungalow in Capistrano Village using the telephone. She put it down gently, Granada, she could go by bus or train but it would take forever. Rob had sounded not desperate, not that, no but uptight. The E-type was the best option and it would give them mobility. She had no idea why Rob was in Granada but she knew the city well. She ran down the road to No 79 glad to find none of the other girls were there. It had certainly been handy, Maria was on duty at the Nerja Club and had delivered Rob's message straight away. She packed a small suitcase for herself. Took all the money she had and was out the door within ten minutes, having left a note for Concetta that she had gone to Granada.

The local bus to Malaga ran every ten minutes so she did not have long to wait. She got off at Torre del Mar and walked the mile to the farm.

In just under an hour from telephoning Rob she was sat in the E-type. *Concentrate* she told herself. *Choke to the top, switch on the ignition; wait until the pump stops clicking press the starter button.* The engine turned but did not fire. She tried again, and again. 'Now wait' she said out loud. 'I must have done something wrong. Hold the choke to the top' she wondered *did I do that last time or did I push it and leave it?* This time she held it, switched on the ignition there were only a couple of clicks she pressed the button praying and the engine burst into life.

The thirty-seven year old Sean Rice, alias Ray Lewis, a slightly built man of five foot six was sat on the balcony of his flat that overlooked the seafront at Almunecar. He had been feeling pleased with himself for the last few days. That was until he got the telephone call from the Colonel that the stupid Ivans had allowed the Brit agent Nicolson to escape. They had promised to execute him once they had finished the interrogation. But he had broken out, now he would have to deal with Nicolson, he savoured the prospect. He had got rid of the other two Brit agents; it had been so easy he was happy to do it. He had no qualms about bringing the fight onto the Spanish streets. But this Nicolson was becoming personal, and he was proving a slippery customer. He had likely rubbed out Frazer and Nosey and they had been armed to the teeth how had he done it he wondered or had he been lucky? *No you make your own luck in this business* he thought.

The Ivans wanted his help to find Nicolson, there was a healthy reward and they did not mind if he killed him. In fact the Colonel had said they would prefer it. It did not matter to Rice he was just another Brit, but yet he was rather more than that. He was pretty sure he had killed his own uncle, Silver Bell, shot him dead in a Liverpool cemetery. The fact that Bell had been trying to kill Nicolson was academic.

The Ivans had lost him in Granada where would he go? Surely back to the Costa del Sol. Maybe that Flamenco troop leader might know something. He lit a cigarette. On the table to his front was his black notebook in which he kept his contacts. He soon found Fernando Herrera's phone number and dialled it.

'Yes Senor Lewis I do recall and we should be able to help you, in a week or so.'

'Oh! that late.'

'Two of my troop are not available this week, Caroline and Duncan, once they return.'

'That's a pity don't they live in Nerja?'

'Yes, Capistrano Village.'

A grin of easy triumph crossed Rice's face.

Okudzhava was dead; he had died in the night, at his own hand read Hernandez. He had used a cyanide capsule it must have been concealed somewhere on his body. The fear of the man was palpable thought Hernandez when he had told him he would notify the Russian authorities, or was it the threat of a long time in prison. Hernandez had no sympathy for him, or admiration at his suicide, the man had been a killer.

Of the other suspects in the bombing, they had little on the third man so far, but Rice was in the frame. Hernandez wondered if Caroline Gomez might know of Rice. After all he was there during the show. And he owed her a visit, perhaps she might have heard from Nicolson? Within the hour he was driving north in his BMW toward Nerja, and was glad to get out of the office.

At No 79 Capistrano Village, Concetta opened the door. Hernandez showed her his identification before asking where Caroline was.

'Gone to Granada' she said 'come in Capitano I have her note.'

Hernandez read it. 'When do you think she set off?'

'Maria came home for lunch; she said she delivered the message late in the morning.'

'What message, who is Maria?'

'Maria, we share this place with her and Carmen, she was working across the road today at the Nerja Club Hotel.'

'Yes I know it.'

'Maria said it was from a relative and to meet him in Granada called Roberto I think.'

'You don't mean Rob or Robin?'

'I am not sure' said Concetta. 'Funny there was a gringo looking for her only half an hour ago just after I got here.'

'What did he want?'

'I don't know said he was a friend.'

'Did you tell him Caroline had gone to Granada?'

'Yes of course.'

Hernandez took a photo from his inside jacket pocket of Okudzhava and Rice at the villa. He showed it to Concetta pointing at Rice. 'Was this the man?'

'May I?' said Concetta taking the photo for a closer look. 'Yes I think it is. The other one was not nice a Russian, Ruban something.'

'Thank you senorita if you hear from Caroline please implore her to contact me pronto here is my card.'

'Is she in trouble Capitano?'

'No, certainly not but it is to her benefit' said Hernandez thinking she could well be in trouble if Rice got hold of her. In his car he put out an alert on the radio phone to detain Caroline Gomez believed to be heading for Granada area possibly in a red E-type Jaguar. Also that Sean Rice was likely heading for the same area; a warrant was already out for his arrest on charges of murder and terrorism.

Chapter 29

It was near four a.m. when Caroline booked into the Don Gonzalo hotel on the outskirts of Granada, near the Nevada shopping centre. She had stayed there before; it was a clean basic two star hotel, with a small cafeteria. Parking was secluded around the rear which was barely visible from the road. She left her case and Rob's holdall in the room. Outside she walked to the shopping centre from there she caught a bus into the old city that stopped opposite the Cathedral square.

The seventy miles to Granada had been easy although she drove steadily. The car being unfamiliar and she had not driven for a while and it was right hand drive. She kept the speed around sixty. The heavier traffic around Granada was more difficult. Although drivers were polite and gave her lots of room, several waved at her *love this car don't you* she thought.

The bus stopped near the Plaza Bib-Rambla, the square was crowded. She wondered how on earth she would find Rob among this lot.

However Rob had spotted her already, he was sat at a cafe table under the lemon trees that ringed the square. He was resting his leg on a chair, nursing a beer, which he had made last for twenty minutes. It was the fourth cafe he had sat at in the square. He had hobbled back to the first cafe twice to check for messages. He was thinking he should go again when he spotted her getting off the bus and crossing the road. She was dressed in red shorts and a white shirt, her hair pinned back, a bag over her shoulder, and she was looking around. Rob got up and hobbled toward her, she was facing the other way by the time he reached her. He waited for her to turn when she did he said 'Hello.'

Caroline shrieked with delight and put her arms around him.

'Over here' said Rob he had wanted to avoid drawing attention to them. He led her to the cafe by the hand. He scanned the crowd.

She picked up he was wary and the hobbling had been obvious. 'What have you done?' she said softly.

'Twisted my damn ankle. Would you like a drink?'

'Yes I could do with one.'

Rob ordered a small carafe of vino blanco which they shared. 'Better not stop here too long we need to keep moving.'

'You certainly have a different look' said Caroline touching the Alhambra shirt.

'That's a long story; probably don't smell too good either. How did you get here?'

She quickly told him. In ten minutes they had left the Plaza and got a taxi to the hotel.

In the hotel room alone at last they kissed passionately. Rob broke away first. 'Right' he said sitting on a chair. 'I need to get this boot off.' He tried pulling it off; even with Caroline trying as well it would not shift the ankle swollen too much. Too much tugging was not doing the ankle any good either. 'OK' he said sitting back 'we need a good sharp knife and some surgical tape and paracetamol.'

Caroline set off for the shopping centre while Rob waited. He watched her walk away from the window, and stayed there on edge until he saw her return.

'These Flamenco shoes are expensive' said Caroline as between them they cut the right boot away. 'Finally in triumph she held up the two halves.'

'We'll keep it' said Rob 'we can get it repaired.'

'I don't think so' said Caroline dropping the remains in the bin.

Rob examined his ankle, it had ballooned in size. He pressed it gently. 'Don't think there is any break, probably ligaments.'

'We should get a doctor to look at it' said Caroline.

'Maybe,' said Rob. 'first a shower.'

Caroline helped him in the shower as he could put little weight on the right foot.

'Pity you could not come in with me' he said 'but risky in the present condition?'

'I might as well' she said laughing 'look how wet I have got.' She had the definite wet T shirt look and showered after him.

He shaved using his washing kit from the holdall sat on the toilet with the seat down and brushed his teeth.

'What do we do now?' said Caroline from the shower.

'Time to think, that's what we do, think.'

Back with Rob sitting on the bed Caroline strapped up his ankle with the surgical tape under his direction. She also applied antiseptic cream to the cuts on his feet. She had bought him a pair of trainers which felt fine when he tried them even if he could not lace up the right one. He found he could put a little weight on the foot now.

'Rob I'm a bit worried about money' she said as she cleared away the medical things. 'I bought all I had with me but at this rate...'

'I'm as empty of life as a scarecrow's pockets' said Rob.

'Ha, ha you can't catch me like that, The Big Sleep' said Caroline smiling. 'Please be serious?'

'Right but no worries' said Rob grinning 'pass over the holdall and the knife.' With his fingers he felt around the outside skin of the bag until he found the right place. Then carefully slit the stitching open for about six inches feeling inside he withdrew a plastic bag in which was five hundred pounds and five hundred pounds worth of pesetas. 'That should keep us going a while' and he tossed the money to Caroline.

'Wow, we can have a slap up meal tonight' she said grinning. She sat on the bed beside him. 'What do you want to do?'

'What a question' said Rob putting his hand on her bare leg.

'Be serious please.'

'Yes, you're right. I need to work out why the Russians were so hell bent on killing us. I think they would have me if I hadn't got away. It's the 'why' that makes no sense.'

'Have you no idea?'

'Not really' he said 'pass me that pad and pen by the phone.'

Rob wrote down T_ _ _ _ _B. 'what do you think that means?' he said showing her. And then added __at __from Hofdi __the sea. 'And this as well?'

Caroline looked at the two problems. 'There are not many words that start with T and end in B.'

'That is providing it is in English.' He then showed her Judd's note pad. 'This is all Russian as far as I can make out, but my name crops up here and there.'

Caroline took the pad and pen from him and lay on the bed on her front with her legs crossed in the air behind her and started trying to find a word that would fit. Rob lay on his back with Judd's pad. 'Good job you got a double bed' said Rob.

'Yes I thought it might be useful somehow not for word puzzles though.' For fifteen minutes they studied the problems in silence.

'There are plenty of seven letter words beginning with T but I can't think of any ending in B, I thought I was good at word puzzles. What about Judd's notes?' Rob did not answer, she looked across at him he was asleep. She smiled. Slowly as not to disturb him she got up from the bed. Taking the key she went out and down to reception, she asked about a local doctor and booked a table for dinner.

Back in the room she was pleased to find he was still asleep. She studied the problem again sat at the dressing table. She soon got fed up going around in circles. *What do we do?* she thought. *These people are dangerous* what happened to Josette and Derek made her shudder. *Why is he trying to do this on his own?*

At six thirty she woke Rob, and told him dinner would be in an hour.

'Good I could eat a scabby horse' was his reply.

'Well I hope they have something better than that on the menu' and she switched on the TV.

Rob got up and hobbled to the bathroom.

'Rob' shrieked Caroline 'quick, quick...'

He was just washing his hands, *how the hell can I move quickly* he thought. His heart missed a beat had someone got into the room, could he reach the carrier bag in time or get to the knife. Hobbling into the room there was no one other than Caroline to his relief.

'Look, at the TV' said Caroline.

Rob stopped, leaning against the dressing table standing on one leg. There was a male reporter dressed in an overcoat, he looked cold, he was speaking into a microphone in Spanish. 'What am I looking for?' he asked

'Too late boy, it was that Hofdi, I think it was a hotel or something, on there just now.'

'Where was it coming from?'

'Iceland I think' said Caroline.

'Iceland, Iceland! Are you sure?'

It was painful, even with Caroline's help and using the tiny lift for Rob to get down to the restaurant. There were only a few other diners there.

The owner, who did most things other than the cooking, was a small fat man. Caroline knew him a little and he remembered her. She managed to steer the conversation around to Iceland. He did not speak much English but with her Spanish she gleaned enough from him. They ordered dinner fish soup, followed by Rabo de toro, braised bull's tail; 'give you plenty of umph' giggled Caroline.

'What did Sancho Panza have to say?' said Rob.

'Yes I suppose he is a bit of a look alike. In that case who is Don Quixote? Some people say Philip Marlowe was a bit of a Quixote, a dreamer, rescuing the ladies.'

'Seems to me he got into more trouble with them, the

209

ladies that is, what was that femme fatale called in The Big Sleep?'

'Carmen, she was a nasty piece of work in the book. Are you Rob Nicolson a bit of a Don Quixote, a dreamer?'

'Shouldn't think so, I'm not doing a very good job of rescuing damsels in distress am I, you have had to come to my rescue.'

'Oh I don't know' said Caroline 'I think you are doing a pretty good job.'

The vino blanco for the first course arrived, they were interrupted by Sancho who had recommended the wine. He insisted both he and Rob sample it to make sure it was good. Rob found it crisp and refreshing.

'Did he confirm the Hofdi?' said Rob.

'Not sure, I think we will have to wait and get the papers tomorrow watch the TV. I don't think we will learn much tonight.'

'It has to have something to do with it.'

Caroline nodded her agreement. Then the fish soup arrived.

Chapter 30

A bright light woke Rob with a start. For an awful moment he thought he was back in the cell, until he heard Caroline's voice.

'Rob, Rob' her hand was on his thigh shaking him awake. She was sat up in bed.

The sex had been wonderful a few hours ago, gentle unhurried with his ankle not suffering.

'What's the time?' said Rob.

'Three' she said 'are you awake?'

'Yes can't you wait?'

'No, no it's not that lover. The word beginning in T and ending in B, it's been on my mind. Those dashes you wrote down were they on the board you copied the letters from? Because the only word I can come up with of seven letters starting with T and ending with B is Taxicab, it can't be that.'

Rob scratched his head. He looked up at her, *he had no idea what was she talking about.* 'I don't know' he said.

'Well think?'

'What difference does it make?'

She lay down bringing her face close to his. 'If a letter was missing it would make a lot of difference change it completely?'

He snuggled his nose into her hair, he loved the smell of her.'

'Come on Rob think man.'

211

He sighed. 'Now I do think of it there were no dashes.'

'I thought not' said Caroline.

'Can I go back to sleep now?'

'Yes, you sleep get some rest' and she switched out the light.

Waking, Rob felt refreshed even his ankle was no longer throbbing. Daylight was flooding the room even though the curtains were drawn. He reached out for Caroline but found the bed empty. He raised himself on an elbow and looked around the room. She was sat on a chair beside the dressing table her head bent over writing on the pad. She was naked; the curve of her back arching to the curtain of hair obscuring her face Rob found the picture extraordinarily beautiful. He lay back and watched her. Presently, she put down the pen and stretched her arms over her head. She looked over to the bed and smiled when she saw him awake.

'How long have you been watching me?'

'Don't know how long have you been sat there?'

'About an hour, I needed the loo and awake I could not stop thinking about that word.'

'Any luck?'

'I don't know.' She came over to the bed and sat down. ''There are lots if it is only five letters, some no good but well the likes of Topaz, Toxic, Telex, Texas, Toxin.'

'Toxin B some sort of chemical weapon?' said Rob. 'But I doubt it, that lot were not scientists or chemists. Telex B some sort of communication, hmm. Let's have a look.' She passed him the pad he looked over the three pages of her doodling, many words crossed out or rearranged. 'What about Trust B, no that's even worse' he said.

'No, no hang on a minute, yes could be' she said. 'And you an intelligence agent. The Trust don't you remember killed Sidney Reilly.'

'What are you talking about now?'

'Reilly Ace of Spies, it was on the telly man. I watched it this year during the winter break back home.'

'Yes, I have heard of Sydney Reilly so what?'

'The Trust was an organisation Reilly thought had been formed to help the White Russians oust the Bolsheviks during the twenties. But in fact it was started by the Bolsheviks to infiltrate counter-revolutionist groups. They lured Reilly to Russia and killed him. Don't you see the Trust was formed to safeguard the Revolution? Stalin, I think, eventually stood it down, but I don't understand the B.'

Rob sat up in bed. 'Well I do, the B is what it says, number two. Like the EOKA B in Cyprus during 1974, that was the second coming after the original EOKA in the nineteen fifties. This is the second Trust to safeguard the Revolution. All these Russians were hard-liners they are going to try and oust Gorbachev, stop his reforms, it has to be. That's why they have met abroad, why they wanted it kept secret. Has to be, you've solved it.'

Caroline's eyes were shining. She took the pad back and dropped it on the floor. 'I think we should do something else now, if you have the energy old man?'

'I'll give you if I have the energy' and he reached for her. They breakfasted in the room, with the TV on but the international coverage was not good. And even CNN had little about the forthcoming summit. Caroline went out and got several English papers. The *Times* did say the schedule for the Reykjavik summit would be announced shortly.

'Now you think you know what this is all about. What do we do go back to the Consul in Malaga?'

'No, there is something wrong with the system at the Firm. I don't know what it is. I don't trust them. The only people I could are you and Josette. And....' Rob turned away choking up. The reality of Josette's death weighed heavily on him. He had to lock it away. This was the wrong time. He wondered if there would ever be a right time.

Caroline wiped tears away from her face. 'We do nothing then?'

'No' Rob shook his head. 'This could bring about a World crisis; we don't know what that bunch might do. They want to resurrect the Cold War maybe even worse. We have to do something?'

'Do you think our side might be the same?'

Rob looked at her in wonder, how perceptive she was like an oracle or a Sybil. They were always women in ancient times, he smiled at her.

'What' she said 'have I said something daft?'

'Far from it' said Rob 'you are absolutely right, why didn't I think of that? There are vested interests in the West who would want to keep the Cold War going. No doubt some within the Intelligence community as well.' It explained why he and later Josette had gone to Spain looking into the Styles case, while no one with real authority was interested in it and it had all been left to Julie. It was beginning to make sense. 'You see they had to send someone out here they did not rate very highly, me. Josette was good but she was ill, so that was safe. Did they already know about 'Trust B' and were turning a blind eye? And as an insurance policy someone informed the Provos but that had gone wrong surely? Rather like catching a tiger by the tail they can't control.'

'You're a lot better than they think, and so....'

'Yes well that is because you're honest' said Rob.

'No, don't denigrate yourself they hoped you would just sit in the sun.'

'Yes and every time we proposed something there was no enthusiasm.'

'But what do we do now?'

'If we can't trust our side, we must the other side.'

Caroline looked puzzled.

'We tell the Russians what we have found, the ones in charge now. How far is Madrid?'

'Must be about two hundred and fifty miles maybe more, why?'

'We go to the Russian Embassy in Madrid and tell them. If we get going soon we could be there this afternoon.'

'I think you should rest.'

'I can rest when this is over.'

'Well......'

'What's the matter Caroline?'

'There is a doctor coming at eleven.'

'You are joking' said Rob.

Caroline's chin firmed in determination. 'Look Rob Nicolson Intelligence man. You're not very intelligent sometimes if you ask me. What happens if you cannot walk at all? And another thing I'm not driving that car until you do see a doctor.'

This is our first real row not like the previous

misunderstanding thought Rob. *Be considerate you idiot, she's right in some respects.* 'No you are right again. He might be able to make it more comfortable. The important thing at the moment we need to find out when the summit is taking place.'

The doctor was spot on time. Remarkable thought Rob *makes all the difference when you are paying.* The consultation was costing one hundred pounds. At least reflected Rob it was not some student. Rather a man of about fifty, Doctor Alba. He poked and prodded Rob's ankle.

'Does this hurt senor?' he said twisting it.

'Yeeeeees' said Rob flinching.

'Perdone' said Alba. 'Likely ligament damage, you should have an x-ray.'

'No time doctor we need to get to Madrid.'

'OK, up to you get it done there. I will give you a prescription for some strong pain killers. Your strapping is good. Try to keep the weight off it; ice will help with the swelling.'

Alba was closing his bag on the bed and noticed the papers open at a picture of Reagan and Gorbachev. 'Good meeting that will be' he said pointing at the paper.

'Do you know when it is?' said Caroline.

'Yes I think so senorita the tenth, yes it is the tenth.'

'There, plenty of time' said Caroline after Alba had left. 'The seventh today we can go tomorrow.'

'All right' said Rob 'you win but it doesn't pay to delay we don't really know what "Trust B" really intend, but it is likely it has something to do with the summit for maximum impact.'

The day passed in resting. Rob tried some walking which was not a great success. A bucket of ice cubes supplied by Sancho helped with the swelling.

Caroline went out and got a walking stick for Rob returning with one that had a six inch spike on the bottom. 'It's really for picking up rubbish the only one I could find but should help.'

'Handy weapon' said Rob brandishing it as a sword and almost falling over.

In the afternoon they both went down to the car park to check over the E-type. After which Caroline fell asleep on the bed. And Rob checked over the Makarov pistol, the action was smooth enough although it was fairly dirty, he made a mental note to clean it with some car engine oil tomorrow.

Chapter 31

A yellow Ford Escort GT driven by Sean Rice arrived in Granada an hour after Caroline in the E-type. He drove straight to the Alhambra car park. *This was where the thick Ivans had lost Nicolson.* Where the trail had ended, they had not gone into the city looking for him the obvious place he would have gone. Now the trail was stone cold. He would have arranged to meet his tart somewhere.

The two Russians were in a hurry to get away. They paid him ten thousand pounds cash; they were awash these days with oil money the Ivans. It was easy money. He could just leave with it, do nothing *bloody fools.* They were not to know it was personal to Rice. He was determined to kill Nicolson. But now he had to find him.

Put yourself in the other man's boots, what would he do? Run for home? Maybe, but had Nicolson worked out whatever the Ivan's were up to which did not interest Rice. But it had to be driving Nicolson.

He concluded there was no point in going into the old city now. He went to the outskirts and booked into a cheap hotel only three miles from the Don Gonzalo. He telephoned his contacts in the area he wished he had more but his contacts had contacts. Put out his alert. Two Brits man and woman, the woman good looking part Spanish fluent in the language as well. Maybe travelling in an E-type Jaguar a red one. Then he waited and passed the time playing patience.

It was an hour later he got the first call, an Irish Taxi driver working in the area. He had spotted a red E-type in and about the Nevada shopping area earlier in the day. Driven by a good looking woman on her own heading west. That was a lead although still old. But he wondered just how many red E-type's were in the Granada area driven by women. If it was still here he would find it, sniff it out.

Rice drove to the area parked the Escort, and walked around the Nevada shopping precinct. He saw the Don Gonzalo in the distance but did not check it out. His feet were hurting; it felt like he had a blister, he hated walking his feet were sensitive. He went back to his hotel disappointed he would try again tomorrow.

Sean Rice, alias Ray Lewis, had in fact been born Dean Martin Grey in Birmingham. Of a Northern Irish Catholic mother after a brief affair with a Polish con-man who had promised to marry her then left her in the lurch three months pregnant. She had the baby back home in Ireland, home being Andersonstown Belfast. She named him after Dean Martin who she was infatuated with. Back in Ireland his mother only nineteen could not cope with the baby and set off for the USA. The boy was brought up by his uncle and aunt. He was a loner from the start. Although small and wiry he soon became adept with his fists. He was feared and disliked at school and not just by the children.

It was his fighting skills that brought him to the attention of the Provisional IRA, although he had no interest or conviction for "the cause." He killed his first man with a knife at the age of eighteen. An Irish Catholic stool-pigeon run by MI5, he took pleasure in torturing him before slitting his throat. Through the contact gleaned from his victim in MI5 he began playing both sides. He got paid well and enjoyed the work; the best part was inflicting pain.

Chapter 32

5.15 a.m. 7 October Severomorsk, Murmansk, Northern Russian Fleet submarine base.

The Andrey Nevsky, designated by NATO coding Victor III, nuclear attack submarine, lay at Severomorsk jetty four; the gang plank was being removed. Captain Yuri Alexander, wrapped in his fur lined coat against the cold, was glad to see it meant they would soon cast off within minutes. The five Special Forces soldiers with all their kit in containers were now on board. Being stowed in the torpedo compartment the only large space aboard a submarine. They had a cruise of some seventeen hundred miles before them to reach the target and complete the mission. Only Yuri and the soldiers knew their destination. The rest of his twenty-six officers, and seventy-five crew men were ignorant of their destination. Not an unusual situation for them. They no doubt thought it just another cruise to play cat and mouse with western submarines. They might wonder about the soldiers but even that was an occasional occurrence. However once at sea some of the senior officers would expect to be given details of the mission as was normal, that could be tricky for Yuri.

The lines had been cast off; a tug was pulling the seven thousand ton submarine out toward Ara Bay. The moonlight was obscured by high cloud the grey light of dawn would soon mark the beginning of a new day. The casing party having stowed everything away had gone below and reported hatches secured. Only the conning tower party remained.

The tug eased them well away from the dock area before casting off. Yuri saluted the tug captain and ordered slow ahead the huge screw at the stern began to turn, churning the water into white foam.

In five miles they would dive and really be on their way it would be difficult to call them back then, turning west skirting Norwegian territorial waters. The border with Norway was only sixty miles away. At a cruising speed of twenty-five knots they should be off Reykjavick on the 10 October in the early hours of the morning.

Once submerged standing orders required radio silence so they would be harder to contact, but Yuri would still have to overcome the usual timed reports to the ZEVS transmitter at Murmansk. He was confident most of his officers and men would obey his orders. Yet there were perhaps three of his senior officers who would not be brow beaten. He knew they would question everything. They had been trained to watch for signs of any maverick behaviour in the commanding officer. They might become difficult when it became apparent where they were going and what the soldiers were up to.

Chapter 33

8 a.m. 8 October Granada.

Early the next morning Caroline steered Rocinante the E-type out of the Hotel Don Gonzalo's car park. 'Come on Rocinante be good' she had said starting the car.

'You're bonkers how can you call a Jaguar a fast cat, after a ram shackled nag?' laughed Rob.

'Well it is temperamental you have to admit?'

They stopped a few minutes later at a garage to re-fuel. Rob worked out Caroline had used about four gallons the day before, so they put in another twenty litres. 'We will need to refuel again before we get to Madrid' he said.

They did not know the cashier wrote down their number as they drove away. Or that he telephoned Sean Rice with the direction they had taken and that they had asked for a street map of Madrid which they did not stock.

Rob estimated it would take them about five hours to get to the Russian Embassy he had the address at Calle de Velazquez but they would need a street map of the Spanish capital. He could have maybe cut the time to four hours but he did not expect Caroline to drive that fast. They had left before breakfast so they would have to stop for that on the road as well.

The N323 ran north through the foothills of the Sierra

Nevada which brought back memories for Rob of the journey out with Linda only a few brief weeks before. He wondered about the men in the blue Transit. *Well don't beat yourself up about them* he thought they had got what they deserved. Yet he could not dispel the feeling he had been very lucky. He wondered what might happen when that luck runs out. *I'm just a fortunate amateur* he mused.

'Rob I think we have company' said Caroline slowing down.

'What, where?'

'Behind, the police.'

Rob turned to look back, a Citroen of the Guardia Civil was about to overtake them blue lights flashing. It slowed beside them the officer in the passenger seat indicating they should pull over and stop. They then accelerated and pulled in front, both cars stopping on the verge.

'I wonder what they want?' said Rob as Caroline brought the E-type to a stop. One of the officers got out and checked the number plate the other was still in the police car speaking on the radio.

The first officer then came around to Caroline's side she already had the window down, and they started conversing in Spanish.

'He wants to see our passports' Caroline got out finding them amongst their luggage in the back. By which time the second officer had joined them.

'Si' said Caroline several times, as the first officer spoke to her at length.

She lent in the window. 'Rob you're not going to like this, we are being detained and have to go back to Granada.'

'What the hell for?'

'I don't know but they are very insistent.'

'OK we'll follow them back.'

'No afraid not, one of them is going to ride with me and you go in the cop car.'

It took them a few miles to find a junction to turn around and head back to Granada in the opposite direction. An Irish-born taxi driver picked them up as they neared Granada, once they were out of sight he did a u-turn and followed them to the National Police Station at Plaza de los Campos. He then found the nearest telephone and called Rice.

Caroline and Rob were put in separate cells and told someone would see them soon, still with no explanation why they had been stopped.

'Please accept my sincere apologies Senor Nicolson' said Hernandez coming into Rob's cell. 'Idiots, estupido they should not have put you in here, I told them utmost respect.' He led Rob to an interview room where Caroline was already sat nursing a cup of coffee. Rob sat beside her while Hernandez got him a coffee and one for himself. Even so Rob was not in the best of moods having sat in a cell for three hours.

'You are in danger' said Hernandez after he had taken off his jacket and sat opposite them. 'Sean Rice is in the area as far as we know. He killed your colleagues.' He showed them the picture of Rice with Okudzhava, and told them the Russian was dead and the others had left the country. Even Mirkin had got out via Gibraltar that day. 'Of the third man in the car we know little he was a gringo very well dressed in a blue suit.'

'How would they have known who Josette and Derek were?' said Rob.

Hernandez shrugged, 'I do not know Senor.'

'No, another mystery' said Rob.

'Why were you going to Madrid?' said Hernandez 'are you going home?'

No one answered his question; he looked from one to the other.

Caroline folded her arms and looked down at the table. Rob took a drink of his coffee.

'Here in Spain we are often accused of being a police state, the more so under Franco, but I have told.....'

'Rob tell him' burst out Caroline 'we have to trust someone.'

Rob took her hand. 'All right, Hernandez there is a meeting going to take place in Iceland you have......' And Rob told him the whole story.

Hernandez did not interrupt but waited for Rob to finish. When he did Hernandez took his notebook from his jacket pocket hung over his chair back. 'Yes here it is I checked with the air lines after the murder of your colleagues, the Russians getting out. Captain Mikhail Leonov flew to Reykjavik from Barcelona on third of October.'

'He could be an assassin?' said Caroline.

'Any of them could be. Whatever, their aim is to bring Gorbachev down' said Rob

'Maybe more serious' said Hernandez 'President Reagan could be a target. Also the Hofdi, used to be the British Consul building, it is now a hotel that is where the summit is to take place, and it is by the sea.'

'A submarine could land a hit squad at night' said Rob.

'I think you are right it is best to tell the Russians of this plot as you feel you cannot trust your own people.' Hernandez sprang to his feet, went to the door opened it and started shouting.

'What's he doing?' muttered Rob to Caroline.

'By the sound of it he's going to take us to Madrid.'

Twenty minutes later a black BMW with Hernandez driving, Caroline sat in the front, Rob in the back laying across the seats, screeched out of the police station and sped away.

Chapter 34

The speeding BMW was watched by Sean Rice from his Ford Escort. *At bloody last* he thought, he had been sat outside the police station at Plaza de los Campos for three tedious hours, he had smoked ten cigarettes, and drunk black coffee from a flask. From his position he could see the red E-type parked in the police compound at the side of the building. He recognised Caroline in the front of the BMW, and assumed it must be Nicolson in the back, he had no idea who the driver was but he was in plain clothes. He started the Escort and set off after the BMW.

From the start Rice found it difficult to keep up even in the city speed limits which the BMW driver seemed to ignore. When he got onto the N323, even driving at times over one hundred miles per hour he could not catch up. The BMW just disappeared into the distance.

'Damn idiot Wop' he shouted pulling into a lay-by they were nowhere in sight, he had an idea they were going to Madrid but where in the city he had no idea. He thumped the steering wheel in frustration. He wished he had a faster car. He could go onto Madrid but what then? They might go straight to the airport and be gone.

He lit a cigarette to calm himself. Then he began to wonder why they were going to Madrid. Maybe the airport flying home, yet Malaga was closer. Perhaps the British Embassy but there was a Consul in Malaga. He had been lucky up to now. No matter he would track Nicolson down wherever he went and he would pay one day soon.

Driving on he turned around at the next junction and headed back to Granada. About twenty miles from the city he noticed a small car transporter, just for one car, approaching in the opposite direction the car on it caught his attention it was red with a distinctive look. As it passed there was no mistake it was a red E-type. A grin crossed his impish face. It had to be he thought. The Gods were on his side he could not fail. Wherever Nicolson was going that car was bound to follow it was his nemesis. It was such a good lead he had to follow.

Rice turned around again at the next junction and sped after the transporter. He soon caught it up, and as he knew it would be, it was the right registration number.

He eased off dropping back to a safe distance he could control. The transporter could not manage much more than fifty. Even better it pulled into services after an hour. Rice stopped as well, in the boot he rummaged around and found a tracker box, he pretended to admire the E-type stroking its curves with nobody taking any notice he placed the box under the rear bumper. It would be easy now he thought.

He went into the cafeteria and had a meal. When he had finished he returned to the Escort the transporter was gone. He switched on the receiver the signal was good and strong he smiled. He even had time to fill up the Escort before setting off after the transporter.

Chapter 35

As the BMW sped away from the police station with Hernandez driving in his relaxed laid back flat out style, Rob was lying across the back seat to rest his ankle, he grinned wondering what Caroline would make of his driving. A pang of sorrow struck him the last time he had been in a car with Hernandez, Josette had been there. He watched Caroline grab the sides of her seat; this would be a white knuckle ride for her. He had managed to use both rear seat belts to strap himself in.

It was not so bad when they got onto the duel carriageway of the N323 most of the time the BMW was up over one hundred miles per hour, but the road ran straight and the bends were gentle.

'Hernandez do you always drive so fast?' said Caroline.

'Is it too much senorita?'

He held the steering wheel with one hand most of the time and with only three fingers often, Caroline watched with horror. 'Isn't there a speed limit in this country?'

'Ha! Yes of course. But policia auto no' he said patting the steering wheel.

'Are you feeling sick Caroline?' said Rob 'we have had no breakfast Hernandez.'

Caroline nodded.

'Of course' said Hernandez 'we will stop at the next cafeteria. But be aware the Russian Consul closes at seven pm.' The car clock read two-fifteen.

*

The stop for food did not delay them long. Back on the road Hernandez was more restrained keeping the speed around eighty-five. On the N5 motorway heading north Caroline and Rob were more relaxed and both fell asleep. Rob woke once to hear Hernandez speaking on the radio. Later he woke again as they passed the Toledo junction the sign told him it was 100km to Madrid.

'Good you are awake senor' said Hernandez looking in the rear view mirror. 'It is arranged your car is being taken by transporter to your hotel in Madrid. The Gran Versalles a fine hotel a superior room is reserved for you both is that suitable?'

Rob appreciated his candour. 'Yes thank you for being so thoughtful.'

'The car will be safe in the private garage the hotel has and CESID will be picking up the bill. The hotel is not far from the Russian Consul.'

'That's kind of you.'

'The department has also telephoned the Russians to make an appointment for you at five p.m.; we should be good for time.'

Famous last words *we should be good for time* thought Rob when they hit the famous Madrid la hora pico rush hour. Their speed dropped to a crawl. And the Hernandez usual calm exterior began to disappear. 'Look at this estupido' was coupled with waving of hands and shaking fists at other drivers.

Caroline was reduced to hysterics at his antics.

'Senorita we could be late because of this trafico and these pendejo drivers' Hernandez stared at her in bewilderment.

'What's he saying?' said Rob.

'Swearing in Spanish Rob and I'm not about to repeat it.'

As the traffic came to a complete stop Hernandez put the blue light on the roof of the BMW, and steered for the pavement and then onto it. 'Imbecil, make way, mireda yes you' Hernandez was shaking his fist out of the window as pedestrians dived for cover.

It was four minutes to five when the black BMW drew up outside the Russian Consul at Calle de Velazquez in the heart of the city. 'There good timing' said Hernandez beaming.

The doorman led them inside where they were greeted by a young woman who led them to an ante room. 'Someone will see you shortly' she said in accent free English and she stayed with them.

'My name is Maxim Fedova I am second secretary at this Consul you wish to speak with us Capitano?' said Fedova, arriving after five minutes. He was clearly not impressed with the three people before him raising a quizzical eyebrow on first sight. Hernandez he thought a typical machismo CESID Spaniard. Although presentable in his light weight jacket his necktie was undone and loose. The woman was beautiful, but her skirt and blouse were too colourful and she was wearing sandals. The man suffering an injury was in shorts and a T-shirt. Maxim was immaculate even in the Madrid heat he would look cool. He wore a light-weight blue suit, with a Hammer and Sickle lapel badge, white shirt and red tie; his black lace-up shoes were polished to a mirror shine finish. His blonde hair was cut very short.

'Please' he waved in the direction of some plush arm

chairs 'be seated.' Once they were all settled he said. 'What can I do for you?'

'It is rather what we can do for you or more to the point for Russia' said Hernandez. 'But it is this couple's story.'

Rob had been thinking about this meeting on the journey, over and over, how to open. 'Secretary Fedova I work for MI5 and I have discovered a plot which we believe at its root is an attempt to replace Secretary Gorbachev which could take place at the Reykjavik summit.'

'I would think that extremely unlikely' said Fedova with a thin condescending smile.

'Do you know the following people?' continued Rob, 'General Viktor Semyonov, Colonel Boris Antipov, Major Sergi Yuzhin, Captain Mikhail Leonov and others, it may interest you to know have all only a few days ago met on the Costa del Sol to hatch their plot. They call themselves "Trust B".'

'Excuse please' said Fedova holding up a hand 'did you say Trust B?'

'Yes that's right.'

'Please relax a moment' and Fedova left the room, the young woman stayed.

'Hernandez put his thumb up to Rob. Fedova was back a few moments later with a smaller, scruffier man in rolled up shirt sleeves.

'This is Stephan Radtsic can you repeat to him a list of the people you were telling me about please.'

Radtsic KGB thought Rob. Hernandez showed him the list which he had written down and then Radtsic left the room with it.

'Some refreshments are coming' said Fedova.

They are interested then thought Rob.

Minutes later another young woman wheeled in a tea trolley. 'These two ladies will help you' said Fedova who again left the room.

They all had iced tea and waited.

'Good afternoon lady and gentlemen, goodness look at the time it is almost evening so Buena noches. I am Leonard Novikov the Russian Ambassador, you have already met Fedova and Radtsic and I can see Irina and Olga have been looking after you. This is, what can I say, this is rather unusual information for an agent of the British MI5 to bring us. However we can confirm these citizens' he said waving the list Hernandez had written 'have been abroad recently. Also this "Trust B" has been, what shall we say, rumoured back home. Do you have any other evidence other than a list of names?'

'Yes Ambassador' said Hernandez 'flight details of many that left Spain recently not only for Russia but other countries as well. Also some photographs' he said which he took from his jacket pocket and laid them on the table.

'They are not so clear' said Novikov picking one up.

Rodtsic who had come back into the room snatched one of the photographs up and spoke in a brisk manner to Novikov and then hurried away, leaving the photograph.

'This photograph' said Novikov 'do you know who it is?'

'No' said Hernandez 'we could not identify him, who is it?'

'You Mr Nicolson?'

'Afraid not' said Rob.

'Did you not mention something about the sea?' said Novokov.

'Yes there were a few words on the presentation board it read something like blank, blank at blank blank, from Hofdi blank blank the sea.'

'I take it you know Hofdi is the proposed meeting place for the Reykjavik summit?'

'Yes sir' said Rob.

Rodtsic came back and steered Novokov into a corner and spoke animatedly in Russian, and then hurried away again.

'Mr Nicolson it appears on behalf of my country we owe you our thanks for bringing us this information. Are you staying in the Madrid area? In case we need to contact you?'

'Yes' said Hernandez 'at the Gran Versalles Hotel.'

'For a few days' said Caroline 'Rob needs to have his ankle x-rayed.'

'A skiing accident?' said Novokov.

'Something like that' said Rob. 'It has been a long day Ambassador, thank you for the refreshments.'

'Of course you would like to get to your hotel.' Novokov saw them to the door and their car again expressing his thanks.

It was gone nine p.m. when Hernandez dropped Rob and Caroline at the Gran Versalles. He told Rob he had booked him into the Gregorio Maranon Hospital on Calle de Esquerdo at eleven a.m. to have his x-ray and a consultation and he should take a taxi in the morning. 'Leave yourself an hour all will be good.' He would be busy in the morning but hoped to see them before they left for home.

The hotel shops were still open and they managed to get some underwear, a decent shirt, trousers and jacket for Rob, while Caroline got some cosmetics.

'That bill was a lot' whispered Caroline to Rob as they held hands waiting for the lift. She held the fancy carrier bags in her free hand so that Rob could use his stick.

'You heard what Hernandez said, CESID are picking up the bill. So why not spend a bit?'

In the room Rob ordered room service for a meal and wine, not wanting to bother with the restaurant. They both showered then Caroline dressed Rob's feet. He decided against taping the ankle again as the swelling was much reduced, and he would have no covers over the foot or over either one of them for it was a sultry night.

They had a light meal of pasta and a good red wine. After which they watched the lights of Madrid from the balcony to unwind, both wrapped in the hotel bath robes.

'I have never been in such a posh hotel before that supplies bath robes' said Caroline. 'They are nice and soft.'

'The bathroom's bigger than my flat in Wimbledon' said Rob. 'No, that's a bit of an exaggeration but with the room there can't be much in it.'

'That's home is it?' said Caroline.

'Yes but I haven't spent much time there over the last year I suppose, and then it got trashed.'

'What burglars?'

'Nothing as nice as good honest burglars it was the result of another case.'

'Oh! Right.'

'Where do you live when you are in Wales?'

'Brecon with mum and dad.'

'I know it' said Rob 'I spent some time up in the beacons training with the commandos, lovely country. Mind you the pubs are different they all stop speaking when you walk in.'

He expected Caroline to comment but she said nothing. 'You must spend most of your time in Spain?'

Caroline nodded but to Rob seemed distracted.

'Not much of a life' said Rob 'a lack of ties.'

'Well I like it and it's better than yours Mr MI5 agent, at least people aren't trying to kill me.'

He noticed that determined set of her chin. 'That's true, but I have an idea to escape to disappear. I have seen too many people die, it builds up.'

'Shall we take the wine inside?' said Caroline. 'Leave the balcony door open and the curtains please I like the lights, they look friendly.'

They sat on the bed, resting against the headboard savouring the last of the wine. They were silent for a few minutes.

'Rob what is your idea, or is it a Don Quixote dream?'

'A dream,' Rob considered this 'no I don't think so.'

'Come on then man tell me?'

'Ah! Now it's not as simple as that, if I do that you will be part of the dream, which has consequences.' He took Caroline's empty wine glass and put it with his on the bedside cabinet, then took her in his arms. 'Are you sure you want to do that, this is a real commitment?'

'What for better or worse, you do love me?'

'Yes I do very much, the real deal in church if you like?'

'I loved you from the moment I first saw you. Church doesn't bother me so what is the dream?'

'What, when I was drunk?'

'No on the dance floor at the Nerja Club you great lummox, are you going to tell me about this dream?'

'Do you know the country around the Wye River the

border land between England and Wales?'

'Yes my cousin farms around there.'

'I thought about a second hand book shop in one of those little towns.'

'How wonderful I can't think of anything better. Have you got the money? Oh! How mercenary that sounds?'

'No it isn't, it is a factor, as it happens I have quite a bit. Back pay to come, my flat and my Aunt, she was called Carolyn lived in Cornwall died two years ago left me a good legacy. So money's not a problem. Although the shop has to be a proper business, needs to make a good profit to keep us. There what do you think?'

'That's the strangest marriage proposal I have had, but the best. And yes I want to be in your dream.'

'Good that's all settled' said Rob and began undoing the belt of her robe. 'I think we should dispense with these now.'

'I thought you would never ask' said Caroline wriggling free of her robe.

Chapter 36

The bed side clock said eight-thirty Rob could hear the traffic outside. He had slept like a log. By the sound of her breathing Caroline was still asleep. He got up and gently closed the balcony door.

He slipped on his trousers and dressing gown and trainers. Rather than use the phone and risk waking Caroline he took his walking stick, the lift was just around the corner from their room which he took down to reception and ordered some flowers to arrive with breakfast.

'Senor Nicolson' called the receptionist as he was moving away 'telephone for you' she said pointing at the phone on the end of the counter.'

'So you woke up' said Rob thinking it would be Caroline.

'Nicolson is that you?' said a familiar voice.

Lanyon thought Rob *how has he found me?* 'Major what can I do for you?'

'Grand, caught you at last. Look it's not good to speak on this line. Get over to the British Embassy soonest we can use their facilities. I'll let them know you are on the way. Be careful watch your back.' And his voice was replaced by the dialling tone.

'Balls to you' said Rob replacing the receiver.

'Pardone' said the receptionist.

'All's good' said Rob and hobbled away to the lift.

'Where have you been I was beginning to get worried?'

said Caroline who was still in bed.

'It took a bit longer than I anticipated. Let's order breakfast.'

'What took longer?' said Caroline.

'You'll see' said Rob stripping off and getting back into bed, he had to give the florist a few minutes.

Half an hour later they were eating breakfast, Caroline had cereals and fruit, Rob scrambled eggs, sausages and toast, and the flowers were right on time.

'What an old romantic you are' she said 'they are beautiful now I'll have to find a vase for them.'

'The delay down at reception wasn't just ordering the flowers' said Rob 'Major Lanyon caught me on the phone, my boss at the Firm.'

'Well about time too, did you tell him you're going to resign?'

'Just forget that a moment, how did he know we were here?'

Caroline stared at him across the little table where they were having breakfast out on the balcony. 'What does it mean?'

'Exactly, I don't know. He wants me to go to the British Embassy here in Madrid and contact him.'

'Hmm, you're not happy about that?'

'No, but I don't have much choice.'

'Josette and Derek were killed after going to the Consul in Malaga' said Caroline.

'Still I will have to go there all the same, but I'll let him sweat a bit. I have the hospital appointment at eleven, keep that one first.'

'I'm not staying here on my own' said Caroline.

'Of course not' said Rob 'you come with me.'

While Caroline was in the shower Rob got the Makarov out of his holdall, the knife was there as well but he decided against taking that and left it in the bag which he shoved under the bed. He cocked the weapon and released the magazine, from which he ejected the eight rounds and with some tissues started wiping the rounds on the dressing table.

'I didn't think you had a gun' said Caroline coming out of the shower a towel around her.

'I got this one off one of the guards when I got away, it's a Russian job, I just think we might need some insurance.'

'Why it's over isn't it?'

'No, Rice is still out there, CESID and Hernandez are looking for him he's dangerous. Even Lanyon told me to be careful.'

'Well he was being...'

'It's insurance Caroline just that, the goon didn't keep it very clean' he said wiping the exterior with paper. 'Could do with some light oil or cleaning fluid the mechanism isn't very smooth.'

'What about nail polish remover?'

'Might do the trick' said Rob. With that and a blob of moisturising cream he got the action working much better.

At ten-fifteen they took a taxi to the Gregorio Maranon Hospital for Rob's appointment where he was treated like royalty. The X-ray confirmed no break but ligament damage. The staff provided him with a firmer elastic bandage to give better support, their advice to take it easy 'time would do the rest.'

It was near noon by the time they reached Her Majesty's

British Embassy at Torre Espacio. They were only in a reception room with a picture of the Queen on the wall five minutes before to Rob's surprise Lanyon walked in the door. He had not said he was in Madrid. Rob had expected to use the teleprinter or secure phone line to communicate. He was the same as ever, no adjustment for the heat, same pin striped blue three piece suit. Rob wondered just how many he had envisaging four identical suits in the man's wardrobe, like a kit muster.

'I'm surprised to see you here Major' said Rob after he introduced Caroline.

'Yes well events have rather dictated, Nicolson I think we should speak in private?'

'I don't see why' said Rob.

'Oh! Go on Rob I will be all right here' said Caroline.

'I will see to it they send you some refreshment Miss Gomez' said Lanyon.

'Just a glass of water would be nice.'

'Are you OK?' said Rob.

'Go on Rob, just go or we'll never get out of here.'

It was straight away evident to Rob, Lanyon was happier in what looked like an interview room, he had a desk he could sit behind, and to dominate proceedings. *Fat chance of that* thought Rob.

'Sit down Nicolson.'

Rob remained standing and went to the window that looked out over some gardens; the lawns were quite brown after the long hot summer. He turned and leant against the window sill facing Lanyon.

'As you wish,' said Lanyon 'make your report Nicolson.'

'Where from?'

'The beginning damn it man.'

'I take it from my arrival in Spain you know the rest?'

'Yes, yes of course.'

'I have trouble with that; do you already know the rest? And another point how did you know I was in Madrid, I never reported that?'

'We asked CESID if they knew where you were and they told us, also that Sean Rice was out there and he was responsible for blowing up Taylor and Randall.'

'Not just him the Russian dissidents were in on it, Okudzhava, they caught him but he committed suicide in the CESID custody, and then there is the third man in a blue suit seen in the same car' Rob inclined his head toward Lanyon's suit.

'Nicolson you are supposed to be making your report.'

'Am I?' said Rob 'the trouble is Major I don't trust you. It seems all the way along our movements have been known by the other side whoever the other side is. Two thugs, said to be Provo's tried to kill me and Linda Styles on the way out here. Just how did they know about my travel plans Major?'

'Unfortunate that, the Gower Street HQ is watched they must have been alerted when you left, bad luck. Followed you and bugged your motor on route. I can assure you your car was clean when it left the Firm's garage.'

'But why follow me in the first place am I that important, was I some sort of decoy Major?'

'No of course not, but we are on the front line every day.'

'How come, Major, this Sean Rice was working with the Russians, I took pictures of him talking with Okudzhava at the villa. Captain Hernandez of the CESID has them. He thinks he is working for the Russians and possibly someone at home in the UK as well. There are vested interests that don't want Gorbachev to reform Russia, are they working with the Trust B. They sent him in to deal with us, but who are they Major?'

'You are assuming a lot Nicolson' said Lanyon lamely. For the first time since Rob had known him he looked bewildered.

'What else should I think? You told me I was not your choice for this job so why give it to me in the first place. Then you send out Josette Taylor still recovering. You might just as well have put a gun to her head and pulled the trigger. And Derek Randall whose idea was that? Granted he had an encyclopaedic knowledge of the Russian Intelligence services but as a field agent he was a bloody liability. No we have been set up by our own side. There had to be a response to Commander Styles's death, so send out a couple of lame-ducks. But we did a lot better than expected.'

'But who would do such a thing you're barking up the wrong tree Nicolson?'

'You told me the Firm was doing Six a favour I think you should start there. Is it in someone's interest to keep the cold war going Major, think about that? Now I'm going back to the hotel and will make plans to go home in a few days, and by the way I resign.'

'What about your report Nicolson, and we will need your resignation in writing.'

'Oh! Come on Major what is the point?' said Rob and left the room.

Back at the reception room he found Caroline gone. The

doorman told him she had left in a taxi he had called for her only ten minutes ago but she had left a note for him. 'Taxi for you sir?' he said.

'Yes please' said Rob unfolding the note.

'Sorry lover
I have been sick, not feeling too good don't know what it is, going back to the hotel to go to bed. See you there. Love Caroline XXXXX

Wish she had waited or called me thought Rob. In a few minutes he was in a taxi heading back to the hotel.

Lanyon sat at the desk for a few minutes staring into space. Could Nicolson be right, had they been set-up by their own side? It had been Six who had given the Styles case a low priority even when it appeared they were on to something.

He got up buttoned his jacket and with a thin file clamped under his left arm walked smartly to the embassy's secure communications room. There he put a call through to MI5 HQ at Gower Street.

'Norm how is Spain?' the Directors voice was clear and crisp.

Lanyon was glad he had caught Leo Hawthorne at his desk. He told him what he had learnt so far.

'Sounds like a bit of a balls-up Norm.'

'Rather more than that I think Director. Nicolson seems to think we have been set-up and by our own side. I'm inclined to agree with him. He has put in his resignation.'

'Hardly seems likely, but we cannot afford to lose men like him' said Hawthorne.'And Taylor dead as well. There are people at Six who certainly would like the Cold War to go on. We know they hate the KGB, but at the same time without them the game would be over. And ask yourself just who came up with the idea to send Derek Randall out here. The man was a brilliant academic expert on the KGB but not a field agent.' Lanyon waited for a reply, he was about to ask if Hawthorne was still there.

'You're right Norm there are hard-liners at Six I would not trust. But this will put the cat among the pigeons Nicolson having gone to the Russians. Think we need to let this run and see who comes out of the rabbit warren. I will take it to C and find out what he has to say. Also I will put someone onto Sean Rice to see who is running him. Good work Norm I'll see you when you get back.'

Chapter 37

The drive back to the hotel was frustrating for Rob; the build up of Madrid traffic around lunch time was as bad as the early evening rush hour. But at last he arrived. The lifts inside the Gran Versalles were busy with a large tour group that had just arrived which added to Rob's irritation. *Typical when you're in a hurry* he thought. In the lift at last he began to get a feeling of foreboding. As he left the lift on the third floor, he thought for a moment he heard a cry, but the landing was deserted as was the corridor as he turned the corner. Reaching their room's door he noticed it was just ajar. Caroline would never have left it open. He straight away was on alert, drawing the Makarov. He knew cocking the weapon would make that familiar metallic noise. But at the same time it was better than just barging in. He flattened himself against the wall next to the door and cocked the gun, pushing the door open with the walking stick.

'You better just slide that weapon along the ground Nicolson, in here. We have been waiting for you. But oh dear, your girl doesn't look so good. Don't be shy Nicolson come in.'

It was a voice Rob did not recognise. It had little accent. It had to be Rice. Hernandez had told him he was ruthless. *Play it cool* he thought. *These psychopaths' like to be superior the moment of power is what drives them, what they live for.*

247

Rob put the gun on the floor and kicked it with his good foot into the room. He switched the walking stick to his right hand and moved to the doorway.

'There you are' said Rice. A slight man grinning through tobacco stained teeth. He stood back beside the bed a good ten feet away from Rob. A .38 long barrelled Colt revolver in his right hand.

Rob's eyes were drawn to Caroline who lay on the floor at his feet, there was blood on the carpet he could not see her face covered by her hair. Her right arm was extended under the bed as was her right leg as if she had been trying to get away. She was not moving, *unconscious* thought Rob. *Don't think about her concentrate on him.* He took two paces into the room shortening the distance.

'That's far enough me buckle, but you are a better target now tut tut, not a good move but never mind. Not that I make a habit of missing. After I kill you I'm going to give your tart a seeing too then I'll kill her. Adios Ni.....'

Lying at Rice's feet Caroline, although grievously hurt swam up through the fog of unconscious to a state of awareness in flashes. She knew the voice she could hear was evil it had taunted her. Under the bed her hand felt for anything, she found Rob's holdall and found the knife. She opened one eye the other was closed with fearful damage inflicted by Rice's pistol barrel as he had whipped it across her face. She could see his feet. Someone else was in the room was it Rob? With all the force she could muster arching her back she drove the knife through Rice's left foot skewering it to the floor.

'Bitch' Rice screamed at the top of his voice he tried to bring the pistol across his chest to fire at Caroline. He was not quick enough. Rob sprang off his good foot holding the walking stick like a lance he drove the six inches of steel spike into Rice's chest. The colt went off in Rice's death grip the bullet burying itself into the floor. Rob came onto his right foot winced with the pain and drove the spike in harder. Rice crumpled dead, his foot still skewered to the floor.

Rob dragged him away from Caroline where he had fallen onto her and threw him on the floor. He kicked the Colt away. He was down on his knees beside her, tempted to cradle her. But his training kicked in. There looked like more than one blow to her head. He checked the pulse at her neck it was steady. He needed experts. He got up and hobbled to the phone.

At the Madrid Central Hospital hours later Rob still refused to leave while Caroline was in intensive care. Hernandez was soon there to help with the details. Even Lanyon turned up saying he had instigated an investigation at the highest level into the whole affair. Rob did not reply. Hernandez drew Lanyon away and they talked a lot, Rob oblivious to them.

It was twelve hours after she had been admitted he was allowed into Caroline's room. Her head was swathed in bandages. She was wired to a monitor and had a drip in her arm. He was told she was stable; she had a degree of brain damage and was in a coma only time would tell what affect that might have. And sadly she had lost the baby.

What a mess thought Rob. That was the sickness she had at the embassy, he doubted she even knew she was pregnant he tried to work out the dates but could not. He was too tired.

'Senor, Senor' a nurse woke Rob it was five in the morning he had fallen asleep in the chair. The side rail of Caroline's bed had been lowered. The nurse had seen a brief flicker of eyelid movement behind her good eye not covered by bandages. 'Senor, Senor hold her hand' said the nurse 'speak to her.'

Rob took her hand it felt warm what a comfort it was to feel her. *What do I say* he thought? *Be upbeat.* 'Caroline no copping out on me you hear me. That bookshop is waiting and this Don Quixote needs you to come back to me.' He rubbed her hand. 'I wonder what titles we should get first some Chandler's I suppose. No copping out for you my girl, no big sleep my lovely.' And with that there was just the slightest pressure from her hand on his.

Epilogue

9 October 1986

TASS the Russian News Agency has reported the nuclear submarine Andrey Nevsky has suffered a fire on board, resulting in the death of eleven crew members, including the captain. The submarine is making its way back to its base at Murmansk from the Atlantic on the surface escorted by two Soviet ships. There has been no loss of contaminated material from the reactor.

13 October 1986

The International News Agency reports the meeting between President Reagan and Secretary Gorbachev at an isolated villa near Reykjavik has ended and that talks have broken down over the US 'Strategic Defence Initiative' known as 'Star Wars.' Good progress was being made on removing ballistic missiles from Europe before the impasse was reached. However the President had invited the Soviet Leader to Washington for further talks.

9 November 1989

The East German Government announced that all GDR citizens can now visit West Germany and West Berlin. Dismantling of the Berlin Wall began in June 1990 and was finished in 1992. The Cold War was over.

Acknowledgements.

Particular thanks go to my wife Margaret for her support in all my writing, and for editing and proof reading skills. Thanks to John Sherress, Iain Ballantyne, Flint Whitlock, and John Mussell for help and encouragement. Thanks to the staff at the Nerja Club Hotel where we spent many happy days. Thanks also to Nikki and Phil at *Vintage and Classic Car Hire* of Melksham in Wiltshire for the loan of their beautiful Series one E-Type Jaguar, surely a star of this book. *info@vintage-classics.co.uk*

The following books I have found useful.
The Raymond Chandler Collection Volume one & two.
Ace of Spies. The true story of Sidney Reilly. Andrew Cook.
The Eyewitness Travel Guide to Spain.
South From Granada Gerald Brenan.
Near and Distant Neighbours. A new history of Soviet Intelligence. Jonathan Haslam.
As I walked out one Midsummer's Morning. Laurie Lee.

Please visit my Amazon Authors Page at www.amazon.co.uk/-/e/B0050CEBE4 reviews are always welcome.

Mark Simmons
Liskeard Cornwall 2019.

Lightning Source UK Ltd.
Milton Keynes UK
UKHW020930171019
351779UK00008B/152/P